I AM DEFIANCE

ALSO BY JENNI L. WALSH

The She Dared Series

Bethany Hamilton

Malala Yousafzai

I AM DEFIANCE

JENNI L. WALSH

Scholastic Press / New York

Library of Congress Cataloging-in-Publication Data available

ISBN 978-1-338-63076-3

1 2020

Printed in the U.S.A. 23
First edition, February 2021

Book design by Maeve Norton

For my kiddos, Kaylee and Devlin,
who inspire me every day.
The mention of dinosaurs is for you, Dev.
And thank you, Kays, for your insights
that brought Tigerlily to life within
the pages of this book.

Chapter 1

The younger girls sit in rows, the whites of their shirts and yellows of their heads reminding me of a field of chamomile flowers. They are Germany's newest blooms.

In matching uniforms, us older girls watch on from behind them, my best friend, Marianne, and I standing side by side.

Today's the twentieth of April. That's our leader Adolf Hitler's birthday. We respectfully call him our Führer. And every year on the Führer's birthday, all of Germany celebrates with parades, with speeches, but also with the induction of the new ten-year-olds into the Hitler Youth for boys and into the Young Maidens for us girls, otherwise known as the League of German

Girls, otherwise known as Jungmädelbund, otherwise simplified to JM. I prefer JM.

The Führer isn't at our specific ceremony in our local München clubhouse, though Marianne had whispered to me about what an honor that'd be. Our leader is off, as always, his location a secret from our English and French enemies so he can continue his important work for our country.

But, of course, there's an enormous portrait of Adolf Hitler on the wood-paneled wall, so it's almost like he's here, and his powerful voice often flows from our radios. He shows himself mostly at rallies, getting everyone talking and excited about his ideas.

As it is, the leader of our JM group, Frau Weber, is currently talking about the importance of what the Führer calls his master race. That means people who are known as Aryans, or people who are racially pure. That can mean blonde hair and blue eyes, like me.

Marianne's eyes are blue, but her hair isn't blonde. It's brown, with braids that reach most of the way down her back. But her hair color is still okay. She's still Aryan, too, because she doesn't have a drop of Jewish blood in her body. Besides, she's very proud that her hair is the exact same shade of brown as Adolf Hitler's.

It's the combination of brown hair and brown eyes that can be the problem, I've been told, because those people are the most likely to have ancestors who were Jewish.

"Those who aren't Aryan like us will only hurt our country and our survival," Frau Weber says now. Behind a podium, she stands before the rows of girls with her neat brown hair and starched jacket. Her blue eyes sweep the room. Beside her, one of our teen leaders, Elisabeth, bobs her head in agreement with each point our JM leader makes.

Frau Weber goes on, "And by sitting here today and pledging your allegiance to Adolf Hitler, you are declaring yourself of German heritage and that you are free of hereditary diseases or disabilities that may hurt the future of our master race."

Frau Weber doesn't specify in this moment, but I know what ailments she means: anyone with mental illnesses, learning disabilities, deformities, paralysis, epilepsy, blindness, deafness . . .

I swallow roughly, trying not to let the action show, because I'm thinking about my sister and *her* disability.

The new inductees sitting before us nod vigorously, as if proclaiming, *Yes! I'm healthy and of pure German blood!*

Beside me, Marianne nods, too.

The movement catches the eye of Elisabeth, who smiles at Marianne from the front of the room. My best friend subtly pokes me with her elbow. I force a smile for her. She relishes praise from our leaders.

It's not that I don't. I like my JM leaders, especially Elisabeth. She's fifteen, closer in age to me than even my own sister, who is eighteen. And Elisabeth seems eager to talk with me in a way that my sister, Angelika, doesn't. In fact, Elisabeth always encourages me to come to her if I have any questions or if I hear or see anything that confuses me.

"We'll talk," she says. "Like friends do. Sometimes it can be hard to talk to our parents or brothers or sisters, you know?"

I only have a papa and a sister. I haven't confided

in Elisabeth yet. But it's as if Elisabeth's in my head. It's as if she knows I have something to hide about my sister. As if she knows I've heard Papa and Angelika secretly talking about things I don't fully understand, their little rendezvous always when they don't think I'm listening, and always ever so quietly.

Loudly, at the ceremony, the new girls stand from their identical green chairs. They recite in unison, chins raised, shoulders back, right arms in the air, "I promise always to do my duty in the League of German Girls, in love and loyalty to the Führer."

I spoke those words two years ago during my own ceremony when I was ten. To be fair, I would've said anything to be part of something beyond my family.

It's not that my family is bad. But my sister is so much older, and feels more mother than sister, without all the coddling I think a mama would do. And with Papa so often at the university, I find myself dawdling away my hours—alone—with only Papa's plants and my tabby cat, Tigerlily, for company.

So when it came time to join JM, I was giddy, my toes

wiggling in my new marching shoes. I wore my new white shirt, my new black necktie, my new blue skirt. It was all gloriously new, new, new.

Being a part of something still feels glorious. I have Marianne, and my JM group, with my other friends like Adelita and Rita. We call them the *itas*. We play games and soccer. There's gossip and giggling. There's volunteering. There are other exciting activities, like ball games and competitions. Those are the reasons I couldn't wait to join. Of course, joining also meant meetings—dare I say, boring meetings—where mostly political things are hammered into our heads about how to spot the Jewish enemy or how there's no need for us to have ambitions beyond "Children, Church, and Kitchen." I've heard it all before at school, for as long as I can remember.

The fact that we're fighting a war is more recent, only three years. When it began, I was nine, but Papa tried to shield me from the newsreels, from the soldiers who returned wounded, from the fact that there were soldiers who'd never return. But after I joined JM, Papa couldn't shield me in the way he wanted to.

Frau Weber was quick to talk about the war. She told us how the Führer was trying to make Germany as big and as great as possible. To do so, he wanted to unify all German-speaking people under one nation. That's why he annexed parts of countries like Czechoslovakia, Austria, and France.

Frau Weber was more than pleased to explain what *annex* meant when I raised my hand. "It means those areas are now a part of Germany. We are one. One nation. One empire. One leader, Adolf Hitler.

"However," she went on at our JM meeting, "some other countries didn't like that. Poland, for example. They attacked us, leaving our Führer no choice but to invade and conquer Poland." Frau Weber shook her head. "Great Britain and France became angry with us, declaring war. It all began with Poland."

When Frau Weber told us girls this, the room was silent.

But my mind was anything but quiet.

Prior to that day, while no one had spoken to me about the war, I *had* overheard Papa and Angelika speaking during one of their late-night talks. Papa didn't believe that Poland attacked first. "Why would such a small military attack our German empire?" he had mused. "I wonder if there's something to the rumors that Hitler only made it *look* like Poland attacked first. I heard claims that he set off his own bombs, because he wanted a *reason* to invade there, where there are hardly any German-speaking people. Hitler only wants more power."

So in our silent clubhouse room, I raised my hand.

"Yes, Brigitte," Frau Weber said in a warm voice.

"Why did the Führer want Poland, though, when there are few Germans there?"

Frau Weber frowned at me.

Marianne looked like she wanted to murder me.

The *itas* looked embarrassed for me.

My question—which I realized, too late, questioned Adolf Hitler—went unanswered.

Because of that day, nearly two years later, I'm slow to ask questions. Elisabeth says I can confide in her, but I just don't know if that's true. All of it makes me uneasy.

I squeeze Marianne's hand, happy to have her next

to me at the ceremony. I haven't confided in her either, only because Marianne would 100 percent make me tell Elisabeth everything I've ever overheard my family say. "Do it right now," she would say in a high-pitched voice. She's hasty like that. "It's our duty," she would add.

Even now, I know she thinks my hand squeeze is from my excitement about our new members and not simply wanting a hand to hold.

With the new girls having spoken their oaths, one by one, they stand in front of Elisabeth to receive a membership certificate, then continue across the front of the room to Frau Weber to shake her hand and receive a personal welcome.

"I want to be a group leader," Marianne whispers, and not for the first time. Our teen leaders are from the older girls' group, called the Bund Deutscher Mädel, known more simply as the BDM. "Elisabeth became a leader when she was fourteen years and ten months old."

I smirk. "I'm surprised you don't know the exact day, too."

“Quiet,” Marianne says playfully. Then more seriously: “That could be us in two years. Don’t you want to lead?”

“Sure.”

But I’m not certain I mean it. I don’t consider myself a leader. Not really. I only agree because Marianne is smiling and I know what she’ll say next: “We’ll lead together.”

And to be honest, I’m at my happiest when we’re together. So I simply reply, “I can barely wait for summer camp.”

“Scavenger hunts,” Marianne says, her eyes widening.

I copycat her eyes. “Gymnastics.”

“Swimming.”

She’s still saying the word when I say, “Crafts.”

And then we’re tossing plans back and forth:

“Campfires.”

“Tents.”

“Hiking.”

Adelita overhears and chimes in with: “Singing.”

We all laugh behind our hands.

Someone shushes us. Marianne quickly checks to

make sure it's just another girl and not a group leader or someone else of importance. She relaxes.

When the ceremony is over and all the girls disperse in high spirits, Elisabeth asks me and Marianne to stay after, to help clean up. Marianne jumps at the chance, and I'm happy to stay and help, too. I feel pride in all the activities I've done as part of our JM group. Frau Weber and Elisabeth say even the little things we do can help the Führer defend our country.

No one has invaded Germany by land and I'm proud of that. There are bombings from English planes in other German cities sometimes, though, but luckily not here in München. So we try to help from afar as our army fights in other countries and while our air force makes their own strikes from the sky.

"Do you think camp will be the same as last time?" Marianne asks me as we relocate the green chairs to the back of the room, returning to our favorite topic. "Or do you think it will be even better?"

I smile. Camp is more than the fun of campfires, tents, hiking, and singing that Marianne and I grinned about.

Camp is freedom. After I joined JM, camp was the first time I traveled without Papa. That summer had been filled with whispers between him and Angelika about her illness, and I was so happy for the break from his worried face, from wondering if I should tell anyone about their hushed conversations. Summer camp was weeks of laughter with Marianne and the *itas*.

"I think camp will be even better than last time," I say. "Remember the twelve-year-olds could pick more of their activities? That'll be us this year." I've been aching for that freedom again. I know Marianne has been, too. She doesn't talk about it, but her family can't afford to travel. While I'm the younger of two, she's the oldest of six, and her mama counts on her to help with just about everything. But at summer camps, the rich and poor are mixed together. Us city kids get to experience the countryside. Plus, Marianne's the only one in her family old enough to go, the twins only nine and the rest of her siblings even younger. JM is my place of belonging. For Marianne, it's her escape.

We finish moving the chairs and Elisabeth hurries us out the door with an approving nod. Marianne gives me a quick hug before we head to our homes, our neighborhoods in opposite directions. As I walk into our apartment, I call, “I’m home.” Tigerlily promptly winds through and around my feet, meowing as she goes. I scoop her up. Papa has all the window shades open, the afternoon sun pouring in, feeding his many, many plants.

Papa’s a professor of biology at the university, but more importantly—to him at least—he’s a botanist.

When I was a tiny thing, I thought his vocation was “potanist” because our apartment overflowed with potted plants. Still, wherever light seeps through the windows, there’s a plant, perfectly placed based on how much sunlight that particular plant needs for its photosynthesis, a process I know entirely too much about.

Papa told me that when I was a baby, he carried me from window to window, soaking up every ounce of sunshine. He said, “Your eyes are so blue they’re almost purple, like the petals of a cornflower. And cornflowers need full sun.”

“Papa?” I say, progressing from the foyer toward the

back kitchen, where I can hear him and Angelika, too. As I near, I realize their words are low and quick, and not entirely happy. Tigerlily wiggles, not wanting to go where I'm taking her. I place her on the ground, and she bounds for a quieter, less hostile-sounding room.

I worry what I'll find in the kitchen. Angelika is spirited and stubborn—she is Papa's tough and resilient petunia. But they usually see eye to eye.

What's got them both so upset?

I wonder if they'll even tell me.

"Papa," I say, announcing myself as I enter the room. A big map is spread out across the table. Towns are circled in red. I hesitate, but I'm too curious not to ask, "What's going on?"

Chapter 2

"Is the ceremony over already?" Papa asks. He glances at a clock over the sink. While his mouth and eyes move, so do his hands, blindly folding the map that was on the table. In seconds, it's nothing but a white square, all its secrets folded away inside.

I nod, my gaze on Papa, trying to hide my interest in that clandestine square. But I feel its presence on the table.

"Sit," he says. "I have something to tell you."

I sit, even though I'd rather stand. In my experience, bad news is only delivered while I'm in a kitchen chair. Case in point, the last time I sat in this chair, Papa told me how Angelika was very sick.

"At first we believed your sister had influenza," he said that time. His skin was ghost white.

My mouth fell open. The flu. Papa has always been terrified of it. When he fought in the Great War, so many soldiers died from the illness. Of course, I knew Angelika had been home sick for what felt like ages, but nobody had told me what was wrong with her yet.

"But what she has is horrible in its own way," Papa said. "Your sister has the polio disease."

I chewed my lip, not knowing much about it but hating that it had *disease* in its name. But I decided on the most important question to start with. "Is she going to be okay?"

"There's so little we know about the disease." Papa released a sigh. "The first recorded outbreak was only fifty years ago. But I'm less afraid of her dying, my cornflower, and more afraid of what her life may be like after she's better again. What all of our lives may be like."

"What do you mean?"

"If she'll be able to walk. If she'll be able to work. How her body may work. Or, rather, how it may *not* work. Brigitte, your sister might be disabled."

I remember how I shifted the chair back and forth

on its uneven legs as he spoke. Angelika was sixteen then. I was ten, only a few months after my induction ceremony. Only a few months after pledging my allegiance to the Führer and his perfect master race.

And there Papa was, telling me that my sister could have a disability for the rest of her life.

"You must tell no one what she has," he said in the most serious voice I'd ever heard him use. "It could be dangerous for us if you do."

I wasn't sure *how*, though. I thought about asking Elisabeth or Marianne, but I was hesitant to ask the wrong thing again. Also, Papa's tone convinced me not to say a word.

So while I was away at camp, pretending I didn't know a thing about Angelika's illness, my sister *claimed* to be at her own BDM summer camp. Instead, she spent months secretly recovering in Switzerland at the home of Uncle Otto, Mama's younger brother. I wished I could've gone, if only to see whether my uncle looked like Mama, like her photographs. Maybe he had a funny way he laughed. Maybe Mama once laughed in that same funny way.

I wouldn't know. Mama and I had only existed on this earth together for mere minutes.

I'd also been sitting in this same chair when Papa told me, "Your mama died while giving us a great gift. You."

But it's hard to feel like a gift. Gifts are supposed to be received, and I feel like all I did was take from Mama. I took everything from her, so I try to take as little as I can from Papa and Angelika.

When my sister returned from Switzerland, the left side of her body was slower to move than the right. At first, she still had trouble walking. But when she focused really hard, her gait improved.

"Things could be much worse," I overheard Papa tell Angelika one night. "We can hide this. So many are left visibly paralyzed."

Still, she cried.

"Will it worsen, though?" she asked. "Is it a disease that can come back, like cancer?"

Come back.

Angelika's disease coming back wasn't a thought I

had entertained. Until that very moment. And how scary it was to think polio could hover over my sister her entire life.

“I don’t know, my petunia,” Papa said, sadness in his voice. “I wish we knew more about the disease, but we don’t. America’s president has it. He’s pushing for research. For answers. But so far . . .”

There was so much about the disease we didn’t know. Except that Papa felt we must hide how Angelika ever had it.

And I wanted to do whatever I could for my sister, including keeping her secret. I liked helping her, and for the first time, I felt like I was doing more giving than taking. But Angelika was stubborn and persistent, telling me I wasn’t allowed to help her walk. She told me she had to conceal the sway all on her own.

Then Papa reminded me again, “Tell no one. Not even Marianne. It’s best to keep our family affairs private.” I knew to trust the sternness of his face, the rigidness of his jaw. And so started my secret-keeping.

“Brigitte,” he says now. This time in our kitchen, his

face isn't stern or rigid but sympathetic. Concerned, even. "It's about your camp this summer."

My head cocks.

Papa says, "They've canceled it."

What? The word echoes in my head: *canceled*. It feels like a bag of rocks is dragging me by my feet to the bottom of a lake—the lake I won't be swimming in this summer.

"Why?" I cry at Papa. Angelika leans against the counter, her expression giving away nothing.

"For your safety, for the safety of all you girls."

I look around the small room, as if I expect to see a bomber plane flying from our range to the fridge. But there haven't been any sirens. No fighting here. No nothing that I know of. I close my eyes, searching for answers behind my eyelids. "But why?" I ask again.

"There haven't been attacks *here*," Papa says, "but there have been elsewhere." He looks away when he says that last word—*elsewhere*—as if there's information he's not telling me. "Many people are wounded. Many people are losing their homes and jobs. Some of them are fleeing south toward us, and many of the youth leagues for girls have disbanded. Those girls have more important things on their minds than summer camp."

His words wound me. Am I shallow for mourning my camp when others are mourning so much more?

We hear about the war front, of course, in our meetings. My papa's too old to fight, but some of the other girls' fathers or older brothers are away, fighting, and it sounds patriotic and a bit noble. But Papa's making it sound like maybe *elsewhere* isn't so distant as it usually seems.

"What about my meetings and activities in the city?" I probe, even though I feel a little selfish for asking.

"They'll continue," Papa says.

But I feel like he leaves something off. I feel like he leaves off . . . *"for now."*

That night, I help Angelika prepare supper, singing softly as I scrub vegetables—*we will continue to march, even if everything shatters*—without realizing I'm doing so.

Angelika goes still, spoon in her right hand. She

rarely uses her left hand, but she can, just not as well and not for as long. "You know, Brigitte, there was a time before all the ugliness."

I want to reply, "Of course, the war's only been going on for a few years." But instead, I keep my mouth shut because Angelika has the look on her face—the one where her lips press together—where I know she's thinking, and then she'll go on. It's best to let her.

"Thankfully the ugliness of combat hasn't come to our city or skies yet." She pauses, a concerned look passing over her face. "But what I mean is that there was a time before the Führer."

I hold back a gasp. What Angelika says is a simple fact. Of course a time existed before Adolf Hitler held power. But still, it somehow feels blasphemous to say such a thing out loud.

"You were only three years old when his face was hung on every wall in school," she continues. "When Jewish people were stripped of their German citizenship. When we were told not to be friends with Jews. When we couldn't even go to school with them anymore. When a Jewish person was told what job they could and could not have. When even those jobs were boycotted. When we started saying 'Heil Hitler!' every day and suddenly there were only Nazi-approved books and Nazi-approved songs." She says the last word pointedly, then she is quiet for one, two, three seconds, before: "You were three, but I was nine. There are things I remember from before."

Angelika stops talking then, and I'm glad. The conversation already feels wrong. It's the kind of thing that Elisabeth says to tell her about. I won't, though, which makes me feel like a bad Nazi. But I also don't want to be a bad sister or daughter.

In the end, I just feel *bad*, and that night I stare at my bedroom ceiling. It's the same white, paint-chipped ceiling I've stared at my whole life. Yet it feels changed to me. Duller.

My head turns involuntarily at the sound of voices, once again hushed, once again coming from Papa and Angelika. I slip my right foot out from beneath Tigerlily's dead weight and I'm on my feet, my nightshirt hitting my ankles as I stand.

I crack open my door. It's enough to catch some of their words. It's how I've learned a little more about how the war is actually going, compared to what they tell us at our JM meetings. I've heard Papa talking about assassination attempts on the Führer and of something called a concentration camp. Papa's words were even more hushed while speaking of those camps, and I couldn't hear enough to know more. But even at meetings, the other girls warn in campfire-type voices that bad behavior can land someone in one of these camps.

Tonight, I want to know as much as I can. I want more than fragments and maps that are swiftly put away when I enter a room. I creep into the hall and toward Papa's study. It's little more than an alcove with a desk.

Their backs are to me. On his desk, between them, I see the map from earlier. A sliver of it, at least. Papa's desk light catches on the red markings.

He shakes his head. "They have gotten closer. I worry about you there, Angelika."

They?

There?

Angelika runs her pointer finger along the map. "Besides the attack on Augsburg three days ago, the British haven't attacked much deeper than our northern coast."

I don't know exactly where Augsburg is, but I know the city isn't far away. The northern coast is far, though. My city of München is in southern Germany.

Papa nods, and I wish I could see his face, because his shoulders are tight. Too tight. "They seem to be doing quick strikes on the bigger factories along the coast, then getting the hell out of there before they're shot down. German planes are superior. Every time the RAF comes inland or farther south, they'll be chased a greater distance to get back to England."

Oh. *They* is the RAF, England's Royal Air Force. They're the ones bombing Germany.

Papa blows out a breath. "It worries me that they took the risk to hit a factory in Augsburg. I can only hope it won't be repeated again soon. That was close enough. Too close. What . . . about an hour by car?"

My mouth drops open at that, at the fact a town about an hour away has been bombed.

Angelika asks, "Do you think they'll come this far inland again?"

"I'm afraid so. They were successful once." Papa draws an imaginary circle around the bombed towns up north. "Like you pointed out, most of the attacks are up here. Augsburg broke that pattern. But Frankfurt is here." Papa moves his finger down toward the center of the map—in the direction of where we are, but only halfway. "I don't see München getting hit before Frankfurt. When there's news of Frankfurt, then . . ." His dropped sentence is followed by the biggest of exhales.

I imagine the circle Papa drew growing and expanding even more, until München is inside the bombs' target. It makes me think of Tigerlily's eyes. I picture her pupils. Right before she's about to pounce on an unsuspecting sock or leap toward the dust mites that fall in the sunlight, the blacks of her eyes grow larger and larger until they take up almost all of her eye. Then, wham!

I shiver at the idea.

Angelika asks, "And what of Ulm? If Augsburg's factory was targeted, couldn't the munitions factory in Ulm be hit, too? Another break in the pattern?"

"I'll worry about you, my petunia. I don't want you sent there. It's so close to Augsburg."

There is the city of Ulm, I realize. Which puts things in even greater perspective. We've been there. Ulm has the tallest church spire in the world. It felt like it took no time to get to Ulm, and Papa just said Ulm is near Augsburg. Which was just bombed.

"But . . ." Papa's arm is around my sister's shoulder then. "We have four months before you leave for Ulm. Maybe the war will be over by then."

"Maybe," Angelika says, but her voice sounds about as confident as Papa's did. "At least I'll only be gone two months."

"Two months," Papa repeats.

And now I know what they're talking about. After aging out of the older BDM group, Angelika wanted to study psychology at Papa's university. Before she was allowed to enroll, though, she was required to do six months with the Reich Labor Service. Every young adult has to participate, starting at eighteen. It means doing things like construction projects or working on a farm to support our country. Angelika was assigned to a local farm. After she was gone, Papa wrung his hands endlessly about whether or not her body could withstand the work. When she came back, she knew her service wasn't completely over. With a glare, she'd mentioned having to do war service work for two months between her spring and winter semesters, too. Her spring semester began today. Time is now ticking for her, and I can tell she's worried.

Angelika asks Papa, "What if I don't go to Ulm?"

Papa pulls her tighter against him. "You know your service is mandatory. If you don't go, it's not the monetary fine I worry about but the Gestapo taking a closer look at you. I won't lose you, too."

What does he mean by that? My chest clenches at his mention of the Gestapo. Why would the secret police—not the ordinary officers who direct city traffic, but Adolf Hitler's top men—care so much about Angelika not doing her two more months of service? Why wouldn't they collect her fine and leave her be? At Tigerlily's lonely cry, I retreat to my bedroom with unknowns whirling through my mind.

Chapter 3

After Papa and Angelika's secret meeting in the alcove, I want to share what I've learned with Marianne. I want to share all of it with her. But Papa's always been so firm about never discussing Angelika with others. And now, after last night, I'm beginning to wonder if Papa sees the permanent effects of Angelika's polio as a *hereditary disease or disability that may hurt the future of the master race.*

I don't see how it's hereditary, meaning something a mother could pass to a child, because she's not sick anymore. But disabled? Maybe. Angelika does have permanent effects, like how she tires quickly. Papa's also not sure if her polio could return one day—and do more than make her left side not work as well as her right. If the disease comes back and makes her sick again, could it leave her paralyzed? Is that why Papa thinks the Gestapo would find it *very interesting* to learn my sister had polio?

It's all these scary unknowns that make me want to talk to my best friend and to hear her confidently say everything is going to be okay.

But all I have is Papa saying in a shaky voice that we'll never know for certain how the Gestapo will react to knowing my sister had this disease. His greatest fear is that Angelika will be seen as both burdensome to our society and at odds with the Führer's pursuit of genetic perfection.

Marianne once asked me why Angelika didn't join the JM until she was twelve. "But she could've at ten?" my best friend pointed out.

She could've. But the Führer didn't make it mandatory to join until 1936. Angelika became a member then, but I don't know why she didn't before. She didn't get sick for four more years. My sister must've had her reasons. But I never asked. I'm beginning to think I should ask more questions.

For now, I search Angelika and Papa's conversation

from last night for something I *can* share with my best friend. She walks beside me, out on one of our urban hikes with our JM group through the English Garden. This is one of our first outdoor trips this season, as the air is just starting to warm and the birds starting to warble. It's more of a park than a backyard garden. A really big park in the middle of our city with monuments and statues, trees and foliage that Papa could gawk at for hours, and glorious streams. I often find myself drawn to the rushing water. Sometimes, Papa lets me swim in it after the August sun warms it, and he says when I'm older, I can try surfing the river. People do, in this spot beneath a bridge where the water moves extra quickly.

It's hard to balance what I see and hear around me—the other girls of my JM group, the chatter of passersby enjoying their Saturday, the melody of the birds, the hum of cars beyond the park—and the fact that other cities in my fatherland are crumbling at the hands of other countries that don't like Adolf Hitler.

Frau Weber and Elisabeth have said so many times that all the Führer wants to do is unite German-speaking people as one nation, with everyone having work and bread, where everyone is healthy, free, and happy.

I think again of the bombed cities and try to imagine homes destroyed, schools gone, jobs lost, people dead. I imagine cities with big empty spaces between buildings. Papa's words—the ones I wasn't supposed to hear—slip into my mind. That this war began because Adolf Hitler went after Poland. And I'm still not sure why he did. Papa said people mainly speak Polish there.

I'd never question Hitler out loud, though. Besides, I'm sure it hurts the Führer to see our country this way.

I finally think of something from Papa and Angelika's conversation I can tell my best friend. I say to Marianne as we pass over a bridge, "My papa was saying that many people from the north are fleeing south because of the bombings."

Marianne stares at the water eddying beneath the footbridge, and I realize, as I bite my lip, it was wrong of me to mention the war. Her papa was drafted last year.

Her head snaps toward me. "My papa should be back soon. He said his duty was for a year, maybe two. He's proud to serve the Führer."

I nod.

Then she says, “Do you think those people will come here?”

“I’m not sure. But I also heard”—I’m sure not to say the word *papa* again—“that JM groups are disbanding in those towns.” I quickly add, “But ours won’t.”

“Good,” she says, and I’m glad, too. Rita and I live in the same neighborhood and thus go to the same school. But Marianne and I don’t attend the same school. JM activities are the only place where we see each other.

“I’m fine with those girls coming here and joining our group,” Marianne adds, “as long as they’re not competition for the group leader spots. Do you think they will be?”

I shrug. We arrive at a part of the stream where the water is perfect for skipping stones. We drop our rucksacks under a tree and join the other girls. But before Marianne starts searching the stones, she tells me she’s thirsty.

Back she goes to her rucksack for her thermos.

When she returns, I immediately know something is wrong. She looks down, her eyes darting. She’s thinking. Then she raises her head, her face serious. "I have to tell you something."

I shield my eyes from the sun. "All right."

She steps closer, both of us facing the water, our shoulders touching. The water sloshes onto the toe-caps of my marching shoes. Though spring is peeking through, it's still cold enough today that we're both wearing our brown climbing jackets. Marianne whispers, "I just opened the wrong rucksack."

"So?"

"So I saw a book, one written by Helen Keller."

In a flash, I face her. "Are you sure?"

"I can read, Brigitte."

I lick my lips. We both know this author is banned. When we were only three years old, thousands and thousands of books that were considered un-German were burned across Germany as part of a huge campaign. Books by Helen Keller were among them. I've never seen a book with her name on it before. I've only ever heard of people like Albert Einstein and Ernest Hemingway, too. I've never seen their books either. I breathe out the words, "In whose rucksack?"

"Adelita's. Her last name was on her canteen." Marianne hisses the words, barely moving her lips.

"You're sure it said *Vogel*?"

Marianne widens her eyes.

"Okay," I say. "You're sure. But how did she even get the book?"

We don't have an answer for that. Nor why she *wants* the book.

Adelita is farther down the river with Rita, skipping rocks like the rest of the girls. She wears our uniform. She attends all our events. Adelita is faster at the sixty-meter run than anyone in our JM group. Her blonde hair is in our normal two braids. Everything she does seems right . . . except for having that book.

Marianne is studying the ground again.

"What?" I say to her. "What are you thinking?"

Our eyes meet. I have to shield them again from the sun. "Should I tell the group leaders?" Marianne asks.

"I don't know. It's Adelita. She's our friend."

Marianne bobs her head. "She is. But I bet Elisabeth would appreciate if I told her."

What she means—what we both know she means—is that it'll show Marianne's commitment. It'll show how she'd make an ideal leader in two years once we enter the BDM. That is, if the war hasn't come to München by that time. I imagine Papa's circle, but I blink it away, not allowing it to grow.

Later, while Angelika and I are cooking supper, part of me wants to tell my sister about the book in Adelita's bag. But I bite my lip. I'm always biting my lip—with Angelika, with Marianne, with Elisabeth.

"Get me those spices," Angelika says.

It's not said unkindly. But in her mama-voice.

I've just finished washing and cooking the potatoes. It's easier for me than for my sister to do these tasks, having to use both hands to scrub and then to drain the heavy pot.

It's not that Angelika can't use both hands, but she prefers to jump in once the potatoes are ready to be cut. Her left hand doesn't get too tired holding them in place. And, if she's sitting, her left hip is just fine.

I hand her the parsley, salt, and black pepper.

"And the onion powder," she says without looking up from her biology textbook. She's using two wooden spoons to keep the book flat.

I get the onion powder, too.

She gets to work, and I watch her. With each chop she makes, her eyes flicking back and forth from her textbook to the potato, I muster the courage to ask her a question. I told myself I was going to ask more questions, didn't I? So I say, "Are you nervous about hiding your disability in Ulm?"

She stops cutting.

My sister twists her lips.

She lets out a breath.

"Yes," Angelika says, meeting my eyes. "I am."

Honestly, I'm shocked she answered me. Papa normally talks around things. He'd say something like, "We all have things to be nervous about, don't we?"

I smile at Angelika and say, "You're really good at cutting and studying at the same time."

She snorts. "Good, I'll be assembling guns and

things at the factory. I'll need my brain and hands working together if I'm going to pull it off."

"Right."

"Yeah."

Angelika chops some more, her lips pressed together, and I know she's running something through that brain of hers. Then she says, "Papa never told you why I have to hide my polio disease, did he?"

I don't want to seem clueless. My sister already treats me like a baby. So I say, "I know the Führer wants to create a master race, and he may not see you as being good enough for it, because of how your disease changed your body."

It sounds cruel, the way I said it. And I didn't mean to be cruel. I'm about to apologize when my sister chuckles.

"Well, you aren't wrong." When she talks again, her tone is more serious. "My body is different. The muscles on my left side get tired quickly and easily. Hitler could say I'm a burden on society. But do you know what Adolf Hitler has actually *done* to people who've had disabilities or who've had mental illnesses, learning disabilities"—she shakes her head—"or who were deformed, or blind, or deaf, or paralyzed? All those people who are so-called burdens?"

"No," I say, and my voice shakes. It actually shakes, because while Elisabeth has told us time and time again of the importance of the Führer's master race, she never talks about what happens to the people who don't fit into the Führer's ideals.

Angelika pauses, like she's changed her mind about answering.

"Please?" I say. "I should know, right?"

"Right." She smiles at me. It's not a happy smile, but as if she's proud of me. "Have I ever told you that I want to have children?"

"No," I say, drawing out the word. Truth be told, we don't talk much. At least, not about futures and having children and all that.

"Well, I do. One day. I'd at least like the possibility of having children." Angelika flicks one of my braids. "Maybe with curls like yours when you were little."

"Papa says I got them from Mama."

"Yeah," my sister says, taking in a breath. "Well, the thing is, there was a time Hitler had people with so-called impurities sterilized. That means they can't have children. Ever."

"Had?" I ask. "Does he still do this?"

"Maybe? Papa thinks Hitler could still be sterilizing people in secret. And if so, Papa is convinced there could be a chance Hitler would try to stop *me* from having children."

I have to sit down, right there in the wobbly kitchen chair where only bad news is delivered. He'd stop my sister from having children?

"But why?"

"Papa found studies of women who got the polio disease while pregnant. There were cases of their babies not surviving or being born paralyzed."

That's horrible, and my stomach rolls. But I concentrate on my sister and the fact she doesn't have the disease *right now.*

"But you're not contagious," I say. "That makes you different than those poor women who were sick and pregnant at the same time." I swallow. "Right?"

Angelika solemnly shakes her head, as if saying, *We don't know.*

We don't know. That's been the problem all along. And I remember Papa's words. Papa's worries, that my sister's polio could count as a *hereditary disease or disability that may hurt the future of the master race.*

I go on, "So it doesn't matter that you're not contagious anymore? It doesn't matter what we know and don't know or what's yet to be proven or disproven . . . You'd probably be seen as a risk to the next generation?"

I already know the answers to all these questions, but it feels important to say the words. To take them from inside my head, where make-believe exists, and speak them aloud into the real world. A world that I'm beginning to understand is different than I've been told.

Chapter 4

At our next JM meeting after school on Monday, I'm still rattled from the conversation with my sister about what the Führer is willing to do to create the next generation of Germans.

We're mending Hitler Youth uniforms while Elisabeth tells us how our boys are willing to risk their lives for the Führer. She says we must do all we can to support them. "The Jews," Elisabeth goes on, "want to hurt our boys. It's the Jews who provoke this war and keep it going."

I find myself itchy. I'm constantly putting down my sewing materials to scratch my arm or the back of my neck. When I begin sewing again, I jab my finger. I suck on the dot of blood while my eyes travel the room, with its wood-paneled walls and the huge portrait of Adolf Hitler.

We sit in a circle in our green chairs, Elisabeth standing in the middle, her body turning to address all of us.

But *all of us*, I realize with a start, sticking myself again with my needle, doesn't include Adelita.

Adelita Vogel isn't here.

The four of us—Marianne, me, Rita, Adelita—always sit in that same order.

But Adelita's chair is empty.

I glance at Adolf Hitler on the wall, as if he knows what's happened to her.

Marianne and I exchange unspoken words, both noting Adelita's absence. My neck starts to itch again. Why isn't Adelita at our meeting? Has she ever missed one? I know the answer is no.

Elisabeth leaves the middle of our chair circle, only to return with a small wastebasket. She places it at her feet. From the trash can she pulls a book.

Adelita's book.

I just about swallow my tongue.

There, clear as day on the cover, is the author's name: Helen Keller.

"This *banned* book has come to my attention," Elisabeth says.

I resist the strong urge to look in Marianne's direction. Instead, I grip the uniform I'm mending so tightly I'm afraid my knuckles may burst through my skin.

"Tell me, girls, what do we do to books like this one?"

On any other day, Marianne's hand would shoot into the air. Today, I feel her tense beside me.

Another girl provides the correct answer: We burn it.

Frau Weber watches, a look of satisfaction on her face, as Elisabeth does just that, lighting a match, and holding it to the book's corner. The flame catches. Elisabeth quickly blows out the match before her fingers burn.

In the middle of our circle, Elisabeth raises the smoking book.

In response, each and every girl in the circle raises her right arm and proclaims, "Heil Hitler!"

I do it, too. There's no way I wouldn't. I'm too scared not to.

After the meeting is over, I return home, the smell

of the burnt book lingering in my nostrils. Tigerlily greets me at the door with her comforting *meow* and the normalcy of her rubbing against my legs. "Hello, pretty girl," I say to her, "I hope your afternoon was better than—"

Out of nowhere, there's Angelika stumbling down the hall. Tigerlily startles, jumping nearly a foot into the air. She lands, her raised fur making her body twice its size, and scurries in the direction of my bedroom.

Angelika continues toward me. Her limp is pronounced. It never is. Angelika secretly does physical therapy at home to strengthen her muscles. But—now—in her haste, it's like her muscles have forgotten.

Seeing her disability so clearly is like a siren in my head. But we're in our home, I remind myself. She's safe here. There's no one to strap her to a cold metal table to perform a cold-blooded operation. She's not standing in the middle of green chairs. I count to three, filling my nose with the smell of Papa's flowers, and calmly say, "You're home from university early."

Angelika taps a rolled-up newspaper against her left leg. "I thought you were Papa."

As if her words conjure him, his key jingles in the door. I save him the trouble and turn the knob.

"Girls?" There's confusion in his voice at both of us being in the foyer.

Angelika's hand trembles as she holds up the newsprint. She looks over the top of my head. She looks only at Papa. I can't help feeling hurt by this, after she spoke to me openly while we made supper last night.

"Okay, Angelika," he says. Now there's concern in his voice. "Let's talk in the kitchen."

She turns on her heel, her body wobbling.

Papa follows, kissing my forehead as he passes me.

I follow them both.

Angelika slumps into a chair. Her eyes blur with tears. All she says is "The Vogels."

Vogels? My throat tightens and the acrid smell in my nose returns. "Adelita?" I ask.

No one answers me.

"Let me see," Papa says, and moves to read the newspaper over her shoulder.

I position myself over her other shoulder.

I see REMOVAL OF THE ENEMIES OF THE REICH.

I read DACHAU CONCENTRATION CAMP.

"A detention center?" I ask.

Papa runs a hand through his graying hair. It was once as blond as mine.

Still, no one answers me.

"I saw the newspaper at the university," Angelika says. "I asked around."

"Angelika," he scolds.

My sister says, "I was discreet. I had to know."

Papa sighs. "And?"

"Somehow the Gestapo found out they had a secret reading circle."

I gasp. "We burned one of their books today."

Papa and Angelika finally notice me. Papa breathes deeply. Angelika twists in her chair to see me behind her. "What?" she asks.

"At JM, Elisabeth made this big display of burning a book by Helen Keller. And Adelita . . . Adelita was missing from the meeting today."

"But how did Elisabeth even get her hands on the book?" Papa wants to know.

I flinch. Marianne.

It hurts too much to think that Marianne told on Adelita. I'm relieved when I hear the distraction of my sister's voice. "It doesn't matter how they found out about the books. The books aren't even the biggest deal, only kindling. The Vogels actually got in trouble because it was found out they are communists."

I've seen that word on posters. I've heard it at school and at meetings. But I still find it confusing. I ask.

Papa hesitates, but then answers me. "Communists believe the people of the country should work together for common goals. Hitler doesn't think it can work. He believes in fascism and insists we need a strong leader to lead. *Him.*"

The Vogels didn't want Hitler as their leader? Adelita may've had a banned book, but Adelita is in JM. Her brother Peter is in the Hitler Youth. Her other brother, Paul, who is Angelika's age, goes to university, too. Sure, he didn't volunteer for Hitler's army, but he also hadn't been drafted yet. And their papa, he was too old to be drafted. But he fought in the Great War.

He fought alongside Adolf Hitler himself in that war.

I'm confused. I ask, "They were taken to a detention center?"

Papa knows my emphasis on the words *detention center* is the question.

"It's a reeducation center," Papa says, sitting across from my sister at the table. But as he says it, I know he's not telling me something.

The shake of Angelika's head confirms my suspicion.

None of my friends have ever been taken away. Though I do remember that our neighbor Herr Meyer vanished for a few months. But he came back. Herr Meyer wouldn't talk about where he went. Another of our neighbors, Frau Roth, asked him. I had overheard them while getting the mail. But Herr Meyer wouldn't say a peep. He also seemed jumpy. And thinner. Had he gone to one of these reeducation centers?

I ask Papa, "How long will the Vogels be there?"

I don't want to sit, but I press my fingertips against the table for support while I wait for either Papa or Angelika to answer me.

Papa shoots my sister a warning look. I'm not sure what he's warning, but I've seen *the look* before.

Angelika stands from the table, her chair making an ugly sound, and she begins to walk about the kitchen. Then she shakes her head again and says, "They aren't coming back, Brigitte. Some people used to. But most don't. Not anymore. I know Papa wants to shield you. But Paul and his dad aren't going to be reeducated. They'll probably die there. Just like Johanna, if she was taken to a camp."

Johanna, my mind repeats as I lean into my fingertips. She was my sister's best friend. What she looked like is blurry in my head. Dark hair. Dark eyes. I know that. And I remember one day she stopped coming over to our house. I never knew where she went. Nor did I ask, because I didn't want to make Angelika cry more than she already was.

"Is that what happened to her?" I ask, my words barely more than a whisper. "Did she go to a camp?"

"I don't know." My sister shakes her head, so much sadness in her eyes. "I never saw her again after

Kristallnacht. Her father was taken that night. I know that. But Johanna, she vanished, too. If she fled with her mama, she never said goodbye."

I don't really remember Kristallnacht. I was eight and it happened during the nighttime. It became known as the Night of Broken Glass because thousands and thousands of Jewish shops and homes were looted and their windows shattered. Jewish men were not only ripped from their homes but also ripped from their families and from München entirely. Where these men went, I hadn't known. I hadn't asked.

For me, that night has only existed in memories created by the words and pictures of others, and from having overheard Papa and Angelika talking late at night. I imagined shards of clear glass on a black background. I imagined the reds and oranges of burning synagogues. And the blue of tears and a blur of bodies being led away. I pictured darkness and violence.

Then, after I joined JM, Elisabeth spoke of Kristallnacht, and how the Führer believed this removal of Jews was and still is necessary. He calls them germs. In a meeting, Elisabeth once used a pointer to highlight the facial characteristics of a Jew so we could report one if we saw one.

But the number of Jewish people in München was becoming fewer and fewer. When Hitler came to power, there were around ten thousand Jews in our city. Soon, after the Night of Broken Glass, that number was cut in half. And powerful men began talking about Jews having to wear armbands with yellow stars on them. These stars would identify them. It wasn't long before these stars were mandatory.

Yet we were instructed never to acknowledge a person wearing a yellow star. Don't talk to them. Don't touch them. They aren't real Germans. They aren't even fully human. *Subhuman* was the term used.

I was told this by my teachers, by my group leaders. But not by Papa. Not by Angelika either. Still, I accepted without question what I heard so often. A Jewish person was all but invisible to me. Maybe this is why I can't recall when more and more Jews began to disappear. I already didn't *see* them.

But I did notice when Johanna disappeared.

Was she taken?

Did she flee?

Did she go into hiding?

Was she deported out of Germany?

Just thinking the questions makes my insides feel weird. And the idea of Johanna being thrown in a camp to die tightens my throat. It puts tears in my eyes, because what I remember most about Johanna wasn't her heritage, like I was taught to focus on, but her laughter.

I once heard Papa warn my sister and Johanna not to be open with their friendship. They laughed, to the point of cackling, whenever they were together. Never in public, though. Jewish kids are sent to separate schools. They aren't allowed to go to movie theaters or the swimming pools or even the parks. So instead, they'd be in my sister's room, I'd be in mine, and I couldn't help smiling simply from listening to them carry on.

I didn't know what that joy felt like for myself until I met Marianne.

Though right now my emotions are all mixed up when it comes to my best friend.

I barely have the courage to ask Papa and Angelika, "Adelita will be sent to the camp, too?"

"No, my cornflower." Papa reaches across the table to lay his hand over mine. "Adelita will likely be taken to a foster family. Or placed with other relatives who are loyal to Hitler."

"Because she fits into his master race?"

"Her heritage and health fit in the eyes of Hitler, yes," Papa says. "They'll want to keep her if she can be taught to remain loyal to Hitler."

My mind whirls, more of my world becoming clearer. And I try to make sense of what I now know, speaking my thoughts aloud. "I know Johanna is gone—" I pause. I won't say *taken* because I want to believe she escaped somewhere safe. "Because she's a Jew. But then there was Herr Meyer . . ."

Papa's eyes go big at my mention of him, as if he didn't know I realized our neighbor went missing for a time.

"And now," I continue, "the Vogels. I didn't think Aryans were at risk."

"Anyone," Angelika says, "who opposes Hitler is at risk of being sent to a camp or to a prison. Anyone who thinks differently, who acts differently, who looks different, whose insides are different. Like me."

"Angelika!" Papa barks.

"She knows, Papa," my sister says, no longer pacing but meeting Papa's gaze. "I told her."

Yes, she told me how the Führer could want her sterilized. My sister would be forever changed. Part of her future would be stolen from her. But she would still be here. I squeeze my eyes closed, a tear escaping down my cheek. What Angelika is saying now, though . . . "They could send you to a camp, too?"

They could take her.

They could rip our family apart.

I've been so naive.

"They won't." Papa stands. With one big arm, he pulls me into him. With his other, he draws Angelika into our shared hug. "We don't know for certain what would happen if Angelika's secret was found out, but it doesn't matter, because they won't ever find out. We just need to be very careful. Hitler has eyes and ears everywhere. We're all spied upon. All of Germany is spied upon."

I never have heard my papa speak this way before. I keep my head against his chest, seeing only the checkers of his blue shirt.

Papa adds, "We'll leave if we have to."

Angelika says, "The Fischers did. They were hiding a Jewish girl beneath a trapdoor. They smuggled her out of Germany."

I feel Papa shake his head. "It's a shame it came to that. They made it?"

"As far as I know."

"That's something. Now, Brigitte"—Papa taps my chin, raising my attention to him—"you understand now why you can't speak of this to anyone, right?"

Hiding Jewish people. Smuggling human beings. Angelika at risk. I look at my sister. "I understand. But why didn't you or Papa ever tell me the truth? The full truth?"

"I don't know. A lot of reasons," Papa says.

Angelika admits, "I know I was scared you'd slip and tell Marianne."

"I wouldn't," I say. "I haven't."

"I know," she said. "But mistakes can happen."

And mistakes, I think, shuddering, could cost my sister her life.

Chapter 5

I have soccer today. But as I'm leaving, I pause at our door, glancing back at Papa, who's sitting by the radio. His words from the other day run through my head: *Hitler has eyes and ears everywhere.*

In the moment, I was so surprised by the Führer's ruthlessness to protect his vision of a master race that I didn't put much thought into the marrow of what Papa said. But I've considered it more, and I've concluded Papa doesn't trust Hitler.

Which is no big *aha*, not really, not with Angelika being someone we don't want the Führer to take notice of. But it also goes against all I've ever learned of the Führer being our savior, our leader. *Führer* literally means *leader.*

But Papa didn't use that title when referring to him. Papa simply used his surname.

Papa hunches by the radio, listening intently to news of the ongoing bombings. For the past few days, our army blitzed various English cities. At the same time, the United Kingdom's RAF has been shelling one of our towns—still in northern Germany—that has aircraft manufacturing facilities and a shipyard. Or at least the town used to have those plants and ships. It's scary to think there can't be much of the buildings left at this point.

Papa's expression is blank, but he rubs his palms up and down his pant legs. Within ten seconds, he repositions himself twice in his chair.

I go back to him and sit across from him. "Papa?"

"Yes, my cornflower?" he answers me, but he doesn't blink his gaze away from the radio. "Are you all right?"

He takes my hand but remains staring at the brown box.

"Papa?"

"So much destruction."

I know Papa's heard—or rather seen—this type of destruction before, when he fought in the Great War.

That much I know. But the specifics of Papa's time spent in the war could fall through my fingers like sand.

Papa looks at me now. "I don't like war. The only good thing war has ever brought me was your mama."

Hearing Mama mentioned makes me want to cup my hands around the thought of her. The details of Mama would pile up and form a great mound—just more and more. "Tell me about her?" I ask as my eyes fall on a photograph of her that we keep on the end table. It's of Mama and Papa from their wedding, a single flower in her hair.

Papa has told me about her before, but he speaks about Mama like he has the hiccups. He'll talk and talk and talk, one memory after another. And then his words are suddenly gone. There's no more, not for a while. And then, at an unexpected time and place . . . *hic*!

This is the first time I've asked him about Mama, though. Normally he starts hiccuping on his own, when the mood strikes him.

"All right," Papa says. "Your mama, she had a touch of rioter in her."

"She what?"

"Remember the word, *rioter*, and find it in the dictionary later," Papa says, and I nod. "At heart," Papa continues, "your mama was feisty and loyal and brave. She was also really hungry on account of food shortages the war caused. The food lines were a mile long. So your mama, what did she do? She balled her hands into fists and she stormed the store. She and some other women did, all different ages. I worked at the shop as a food bagger, and your mama literally ran right into my arms." He laughs. "One look at her fiery eyes and I knew I never wanted to let her go. It wasn't long after that day, though, that I got drafted. One of the happiest moments of my life was when I came back to her." Papa runs his tongue over his teeth, his attention on a spot on the linoleum floor that curls up at the tile's edge.

I let him have a moment, hoping he'll go on.

But then Papa says, "You'll be late for soccer."

I am a few minutes late, which has the benefit of letting me skip the hellos at the beginning of our game, in particular my hello to Marianne. She informed on Adelita. I know it, and it leaves my insides feeling like a volcano, all hot and bubbly, unsure of how to act around her. As Marianne told me, it was her duty to tell. The Vogels are guilty of working against the Nazi Party. They are anti-Nazi. Still, what Marianne did feels wrong. Catastrophically wrong to rip apart a family that way.

Marianne runs down the other side of the soccer field, the ball at her feet. We're on the same team. She sees me, open in front of the net.

"Brigitte!" she calls.

The ball splits two of our opponents and bounces a few times before I catch it against my body. One touch. Another. Then I pull my foot back and release the ball, aiming for the upper corner of the goal.

The goalie stops my shot, and there's a chorus of opposing groans and cheers. Within seconds, Marianne's heavy breathing is at my ear and her arm is slung around me. "We'll get it next time."

She smiles. I smile back. And I'm not sure I'll be able to bring up Adelita Vogel after something so normal, so us.

When I return home, I replace thoughts of Adelita and Marianne with the hope that Papa will pick up with more Mama Hiccups. But he doesn't. In his alcove, I pluck the dictionary from his small library, only two shelves high. *Rioter* isn't listed, but *riot* is: *A tumultuous disturbance of the public peace.*

And I wonder about the word *peace* at a time when so many were hungry. I decide Mama was right to riot. I also wonder if a large part of war is deciding what's wrong, what's right, and if there's a gray area smack-dab in the middle.

Chapter 6

May brings sunshine and warmth, even more chirping birds, extra people out and about. Those are the good things. The bad is the bombings . . . bombings that seem to be dancing all around Frankfurt.

Two of the newly bombed cities are *between* Frankfurt and München. But not Frankfurt. Not yet. Though one of the cities is attacked three nights in a row. I console myself with the detail that neither of these cities is within my state of Bavaria, where München is. These cities are still in other states of Germany.

I console myself the same way again at the end of the month when there's a massive air raid. Horrifyingly massive, targeting over two hundred factories. The death tolls. The numbers of people now without homes. Those details are also horrifyingly scary. This time, the city is in western Germany *above* Frankfurt, farther from München than the other bombings this month.

Maybe they won't come this far south. Maybe Augsburg, so close to us, was a fluke, and München won't be hit. Ulm, where Angelika is going soon, won't be hit.

Still, I think of Papa's imaginary circle.

Even if Frankfurt hasn't been bombed yet, so many cities around it have been. I can't help but feel that his circle is growing.

Each morning, I hold Tigerlily to my chest and amble toward the kitchen. That's where Papa will be with his radio. I bet he has the radio on before he fully clears the sleep from his eyes. The bombings happen overnight. The morning newscast tells us of any new ones. Sometimes the air raids target a single city and sometimes more than one location is blasted in a single night.

Within the four walls of our apartment, Papa always mumbles to himself about all he hears, but as soon as we go outside—as the three of us walk toward the university, with my school only a block farther that I walk on my own—we talk of anything but the war and those bombings.

In June, there's another big one, a major bombing back up north near the coast.

Papa listens to the broadcast, his head shaking. The targets are vast:

A shipbuilding company.

Two shipyards.

An aircraft factory.

A motor transport plant.

An oil refinery.

A steel mill.

A shelter for our submarines.

"So much destruction," Papa says, like he has before.

It feels weird to continue with my day, but I do. School. Homework. JM.

One day, coming home from school, I stop to check the mail. We're on the first floor of a three-story apartment building, our mailboxes on a strip outside. Back inside, I flip through the envelopes, mindlessly walking toward the kitchen. One is addressed not to Papa but to our household. I'll open it then. It contains a folded paper with lots and lots of text. At the top, it reads LEAFLETS OF THE WHITE ROSE. There's a roman numeral one beneath the title. I begin reading, finding it fitting that Papa's roses are currently in bloom. But I'm not sure what I'm reading. And only a few lines in, I scrunch my nose. It says how every honest German should be ashamed of his government.

What?

I look around my kitchen as if someone can explain to me what I'm reading. Instantly, it feels like I should put the letter down and step away. But I'm also curious about what's in my hands. I'll only scan, I decide. I won't read it. Not fully.

I see the mention of the city of Köln and how it's in ruins. That's a town from Papa's radio.

Then I read how the German people should be against fascism.

It's a word I've heard before, even if the meaning doesn't come to me. Papa spoke it; he referred to Hitler as someone who believes in fascism.

Is this flyer not for but *against* the Führer?

I drop the paper as if it's on fire.

It should be on fire.

As quickly as I can, I have the flyer back into the envelope, but I rip the envelope in the process and I curse. I hide the envelope in the middle of the pile of mail. I tell myself I never touched the thing.

During our clubhouse meeting the next day, we girls stand shoulder to shoulder, in three rows, practicing our songs. Between songs, when gossip picks up, I lean toward whatever is being said, certain it'll be about that traitorous flyer. But it's not. No one mentions it.

After Elisabeth claps her hands, telling us we're done using our beautiful voices, I nearly stumble down the steps that lead outside. I'm eager to talk to Marianne. "Did you get anything strange in the mail yesterday?"

"No," she says. "Only a letter from my papa. He's at the Russian Front."

Marianne's family didn't get a copy of the flyer? But mine did. Strange—the type of strange that gives me the shivers. I shake off the feeling and ask, "Your papa's well?"

She smiles. "Yes."

Marianne goes left around a puddle. I go right. When we rejoin, she asks, "Why? Did you get something weird in the mail?"

"I'm not sure," I say. Papa didn't mention the flyer this morning.

Marianne cocks her head, but Rita says, "We sure did."

I jump at her voice. I didn't realize she was behind us. I would have heard her normally, because normally she would've been talking with Adelita. They were inseparable. But now Adelita is gone and the *itas* are no more. My chest tightens at the truth of why and how she's gone. I wonder if Rita knows. If anyone in our group knows the book we burned was Adelita's. If anyone connected the two: the burned book and Adelita's absence since. At our next meeting, Elisabeth only told us that Adelita and her family left München very suddenly.

"I'm sure she'll be back" is all Rita said when I asked her if she was okay.

"Actually," Rita says now, "the mail didn't come to

our apartment, but a flyer was mailed to our beer hall. My papa didn't let me read it, but I heard him whispering to my mama, something about Germany *before* and trying to get us to do something called *passive resistance* to pursue our *freedom*."

Marianne asks, "Freedom from what?"

Rita raises her eyebrows. "Not *what* but *who*."

I know *who*, but I won't say it. I instead busy myself with a honeysuckle bloom that I pluck from a bush in a small sidewalk garden. Even without further clarification, Marianne understands, and her mouth mimics a goldfish: open, closed, open, closed.

Rita says, "Apparently, there was a line at the end of the leaflet about posting it, making copies, or passing it on."

"You didn't dare post it," Marianne snaps.

"Of course not," Rita says, her braids swaying as she shakes her head. "But that's why my papa thinks a copy was sent to us, so we could post it on our bulletin board. He certainly doesn't believe any of it. He called it anti-Nazi propaganda. And he thinks there'll be more of it. Yesterday's flyer had a number one on it."

I pinch the bottom of the honeysuckle and begin to pull free the stamen, a small stem.

"Shameful," Marianne insists. "Good grief, you could get arrested for something like that." Marianne lowers her voice. "Who on earth wrote it?"

Rita offers, "They call themselves the White Rose."

With the stem I pulled free comes a small drop of nectar from the middle of the bloom. I put the stamen on my tongue, the honey taste filling my mouth.

"What does that even mean? White Rose?" Marianne asks. "That's not what you got in the mail, was it, Brigitte?"

It's my turn to be a goldfish, my honeysuckle stem stuck to my lip, as I wonder why my family got one of these dangerous pamphlets. I lie, "Of course not."

Marianne says, "Thank goodness. But then what strange thing did you get?"

I'm at a loss. I hold up my index finger while I fake the buildup and the release of a sneeze. It's not an easy thing to fake.

Marianne blesses my sneeze by saying gesundheit, then asks, "The flowers bothering you?"

Something like that.

"We just got mail that wasn't for us," I say, knowing Marianne will ask again. "It must have been an honest mistake." I'm not sure my lie convinces them.

When I get home, I stare at our mailbox, wondering if yesterday's leaflet will be followed by another one today. I convince myself, yes. And then I convince myself that the mailbox is booby-trapped. I imagine it all. I'll open the box. I'll touch the envelope of Leaflet Number Two, and when I do, my hand will get stuck to it, as if there's invisible glue or as if someone put a magical spell on it. I'll yank my hand out of the mailbox, but the envelope will tag along. No level of shaking or wiggling or wrenching will get the thing off. Then everyone will know. They'll all know that *my* family got one of the anti-Nazi pamphlets. They'll think *we* are against the Nazi Party. We'll be taken away, just like the Vogels. I shiver at my colorful foreboding, just as my neighbor says, "Afternoon, Brigitte."

I jump and squeak out a hello.

Frau Roth reaches into the mailbox beside ours, humming. She takes out her mail. "Is Angelika feeling better?" Her smile is so sweet I'm afraid I'll get a cavity.

"What?" I say loudly, too loudly. "Why?"

"Oh, I saw her limping the other day, that's all. I figured she took a tumble. I did myself just the other day when I was going down to the cellar to fetch something."

I lick my lips. "Oh yes, she's all better."

"Did she fall?"

I'm tempted to fake another sneeze. But this lie comes to me quicker. "She did. She was studying really hard while walking down the stairs at the university and she missed a step. But I got her some ice and now she's all fine."

"Such good girls you both are." She grabs my chin, squeezes. "Now you have a good evening, Brigitte."

I mumble a goodbye. After she leaves, I wipe the sweat from my forehead. I'm about to leave, too, then realize . . . the mail. I still haven't gotten it.

But cheery Frau Roth left unscathed from getting her mail. There was nothing that looked troubling inside. No second leaflet.

Though perhaps the White Rose didn't send her anything.

I could simply go inside and let Papa get the mail. But what if there *is* something from the White Rose and someone other than me finds it? No, I need to get the mail. And if there is something unspeakable—and if it doesn't stick to me—I'll get rid of it. Even Papa and Angelika won't know. If I dust it in catnip, it won't stand a chance against Tigerlily.

I count down from three, then as quickly as possible, I grab whatever's in the mailbox. I don't even look. Then I skedaddle inside, like I've just committed a heinous crime—when all I did was get the mail.

Still, I practically run past Frau Roth's closed door and into our apartment. I've never felt happier to be home alone with Tigerlily and our hundred plants. My cat circles me like a shark. I risk looking at the mail in my hands, so completely and utterly relieved when I don't see anything beyond our normal invoices and catalogs.

My plan is to throw the new mail on top of the old mail, but then when I see the pile, I can't seem to go near it. What if Papa didn't look at it and the first White Rose envelope is still there?

What if I stopped acting paranoid? No one is going to jump out at me and scream, "Aha! I caught you red-handed!"

I approach.

The envelope is gone, with its talk of *passive resistance* and *freedom*.

Papa obviously saw the White Rose flyer, unless the bogeyman took it away. Either way, problem solved. It's gone.

That's a relief.

And I tell myself that another one isn't coming.

I take a breath. I have another month of school to go until summer holiday. I'll play soccer. I'll go on hikes. I'll attend our meetings. I'll help Angelika with suppers. Everything will be normal.

But . . . I wonder . . . what does *passive resistance* mean?

We have a dictionary, I remind myself. I looked up *riot* just the other day. Papa encourages me to use the dictionary. But that leaflet wasn't for my eyes.

My legs betray me and I find myself in Papa's alcove.

My hands betray me next, spreading the dictionary out in front of me. And what *passive resistance* means is *a nonviolent opposition to authority*. Opposition to the Führer, I realize.

I hear our apartment door open and I stiffen. I'm not sure how Papa would feel about me not only reading the leaflet but also looking up words from it. I'm as quick as a wink to get that dictionary closed and hurry to my room.

Chapter 7

I *had* a plan. School. Soccer. Hikes. Meetings. Suppers. The thing is, the plan doesn't include another leaflet coming so soon, only days later. I return from a JM event where we collected army donations to find Papa at the table, holding a piece of paper.

I freeze.

Instantly, I see that it has a roman numeral two on it. Papa's bottom lip is between his teeth. He's also pinching his top lip between his thumb and forefinger. He's doing both, as if he can't decide which response is right. Both mean he's uneasy.

"Papa?"

"Brigitte." But then he doesn't say any more. He folds the flyer, puts it in the envelope, then into the breast pocket of his blazer that he hadn't bothered to take off when he came in. “I’ll get the mail from now on, understand?”

I nod. The mention of the mail reminds me of my run-in with Frau Roth, and how she noticed Angelika’s limp.

I tell Papa.

“Thank you, Brigitte. Thank you for telling me. I’ll talk with your sister about being more careful. We all need to be careful.”

Papa’s smile and praise give me confidence to assert myself even more. I decide to be bold and ask, “What were you reading?”

“It’s nothing for your eyes, my cornflower.”

His response stings a bit.

Is the leaflet not for my eyes because Papa thinks the content is blasphemous? I know Papa detests how the Führer would view Angelika, but is Papa otherwise a good German? Does he support the Führer’s other efforts to make our country great? Surely Papa *does.* He’s never said or acted like he doesn’t.

Perhaps Papa simply doesn’t want me reading the flyer because the content is confusing or too violent or too *something*. Maybe he's protecting me, which makes me feel a little prickly . . . but deep down I'm relieved.

The next day at another JM meeting, we're sitting in our circle—Adelita's chair still obviously vacant—and I learn the answer. What's in the leaflet is too real and too shocking.

Rita's family received the second flyer, too. She told Marianne, and Marianne convinced her to tell Elisabeth. Now Rita is in the middle of our circle and Elisabeth and Frau Weber are encouraging—in very demanding tones—that Rita share what the leaflet says.

Rita clutches her hands together as she begins. "Well, the White Rose says that three hundred thousand Jews have been killed since Poland was invaded less than three years ago."

The room is silent. Some girls are expressionless. Some almost look triumphal, with the tiniest of smiles on their faces. Some—like me—look around to see those expressions. I don't dare look at Marianne's beside me. But I try to hide how alarming that sounds. Three hundred thousand Jews have been *killed*?

The stomp of Elisabeth's foot makes us all jump. "It's a horrendous lie."

The girls nod their heads. Marianne's nod is very brisk. I see that. I mimic their reactions. But what if that number of human deaths is true? After all, the Night of Broken Glass happened. Johanna vanished. So many Jews in München were forcefully removed after that night. Still, I've never heard someone—or multiple someones, if more than one person is writing these pamphlets—talk this way.

Elisabeth motions and coaxes Rita to keep revealing the leaflet's words.

I don't think my friend wants to, but she continues, "The leaflet says that any Germans who know the, um, truth . . ." Rita pauses, as if she expects Elisabeth or Frau Weber to snap. But then she says, "They put it out of their minds or make up excuses to justify what the Führer is doing. The White Rose says we are accepting of what's happening instead of showing sympathy." While Rita looks nervous—very, very nervous—she puts emphasis on that last word, on *sympathy*.

Elisabeth's nostrils flare, and I drop my gaze to my

shoes. As Rita goes on, her voice is a higher pitch than usual. "The White Rose . . . well, they say the Nazi Party may not have started bad, but we've become bad."

Elisabeth and Frau Weber explode in unison: "That's enough."

I glance at Rita. She's shrinking away, her head down, her shoulders hunched, her arms pulled tightly across her stomach. I feel for her. She didn't offer up this information. They *asked* for it.

"Sit," Frau Weber demands of Rita.

Rita sits quickly.

Frau Weber motions to Elisabeth, who takes the center of our circle. Elisabeth's smile is tight. "Let us remember what Joseph Goebbels says."

He's Adolf Hitler's propaganda minister.

Elisabeth's gaze moves from face to face. "Yes, a Jew is technically a human being. But think of a flea. It's an animal like any other animal, except it's an unpleasant one. Thus, we have no duty to protect or defend a flea, when all it does is bite and torment us. Rather, we remove the flea, rendering it harmless." Her gaze moves more intently than before. "Now, does anyone have anything else to add? Has any other family received these leaflets?"

One thing is clear: Not another soul will admit their family received the White Rose's propaganda. I wonder if anyone else's family *did*. Or is it only my family, who not only receives the leaflets but also thinks it's horrible to compare a human being to a flea? Johanna was not a flea.

Elisabeth's jaw is tight as her eyes pass over our circle a third time, then a fourth. Elisabeth is like an animal herself, trying to sniff out the very answer to my unspoken questions. And I think I know why . . . she's going to keep her eyes on Rita. My friend's retelling of the leaflet sounded sympathetic. And others who receive it may be equally thoughtful about this new propaganda.

Is Papa?

Once, one of his colleagues from the university said that Papa has a bleeding heart. I was younger and it was a phrase I'd only heard as the name of a plant, but his colleague wasn't talking about plants. And that's why, for days, I watched with fear for signs of red over

Papa's left breast pocket. Angelika caught me staring. And when I told her why, she promptly laughed at me, explaining the expression *a bleeding heart* only meant that Papa was softhearted and sympathetic to others.

Is Papa's bleeding heart why the White Rose targeted us?

I can't imagine Papa could learn of hundreds of thousands of deaths and think of those people as nothing more than fleas.

And now I can't help wondering if there will be a third leaflet, and what new truths will be shared that people like Elisabeth and Frau Weber would rather I not know.

I arrive home from my meeting and I see the mail on the counter. Down the hall, Papa and Angelika are hunched together in his alcove, reading something. Papa's forehead is cradled in his large hand.

It's the third flyer; I know it, as if I conjured it with my thoughts. And the fact there's already a third leaflet is startling.

The second leaflet arrived within three days of the

first. However, this third pamphlet came only twenty-four hours after the second one caused such a stir.

Yesterday, I asked Papa, "What are you reading?" But I already know. This time, what I want to ask is "What does it say?"

Curiosity is like one of Papa's phlox plants. It creeps, the plant does, taking up more of the earth as it grows. When Papa brought a phlox home one day in a pot, he told me the flowering plant isn't native to our country. But it endures in Germany now, too, and I've often watched our plant, imagining the stems to be tiny fingers, slowly gripping the soil as it moves toward the pot's rim. Now the plant dangles over, escaping toward the floor. It hasn't reached yet, but I bet it'll continue to spread once it's there, if it makes it. Tigerlily is endlessly whacking the poor dangling plant with her paws.

All that's to say, I feel as if my curiosity is creeping and growing like a phlox plant. So I do ask, "What does the leaflet say?"

My voice alarms Papa, and he startles. He chuckles at his reaction, but then he licks his lips, exchanging a quick look with my sister. He asks me, "So you've heard of them?"

I smile inwardly that Papa didn't feign confusion or discreetly slide the flyer under a stack of papers he should otherwise be grading. He didn't brush me off, then continue this conversation with Angelika when they both think I'm sleeping. They're including me. Angelika wasn't wrong; Papa has shielded me, as gentle with me as he is with his roses.

"Rita's family gets the leaflets," I say. "At our meeting today, she told us what the second one said."

Papa raises an eyebrow. "And how did your leaders react?"

"Well . . . Elisabeth wants us to tell her if our family receives one or if we know of anyone who does."

It's the first time I've told my papa this . . . that Elisabeth encourages us to tell her what's happening in our homes.

Papa twists his lips now.

"But I didn't tell," I'm quick to add. "I know we got the first two."

Papa nods, but there's something in his eyes I can't

decipher. He taps his finger on the leaflet. "This one talks about sabotage. Essentially what we can do to stop Nazism."

I glance at my sister, and then back to Papa. "Like what?"

"They spoke in general terms, to look for opportunities to disrupt the continuation of the current regime."

Angelika says, "Not purchasing newspapers that support Hitler. Not making donations. Those types of things."

I see.

"But what about you working at the factory next month?" I ask her. "And all that I do with the JM?"

"You must do exactly as you've been doing," Papa says firmly. "And Angelika will go to the factory. First and foremost, we must think of our family. And that means acting as if we support this regime, even if I do not."

He said it. I wondered, and Papa just said it. In truth, his words are paralyzing—suffocating, even—going against all I've ever been told.

Ever since joining the JM, I've come home from

meetings and repeated what I've learned there. Papa never so much as grunted or moaned or skipped a beat.

Had Papa not trusted me to show me his *true* opinions? Did he think I was too young? Or that I'd tell Elisabeth?

Those questions hurt. But what doesn't hurt is that I feel like Papa trusts me *now*.

"I do not support this regime," Papa repeats. But then, as if he's speaking to himself more so than to me and my sister, he says, "But with your mama gone, I'm not in a position to defy this regime either."

My breath hitches at the idea of the Gestapo getting their hands on Papa, leaving my sister and me as orphans.

"All we can do is wait," Papa says, "and pray that as few lives as possible are lost to this war before it's over."

Papa glances toward the living room, toward his radio.

I think of soldiers dying every day. And of the towns being bombed on both sides. I think about the three hundred thousand Jewish lives already taken. And the many who've fled or gone into hiding to save their lives. I can't imagine leaving everything I've ever known.

"I'm sorry about Johanna," I say to my sister.

Her breath hitches. I caught her off guard. She closes her eyes, as if remembering, and Papa palms her shoulder.

"What is it?" I say softly.

"Johanna was so scared," Angelika says. "Hostility against Jewish people didn't start with Hitler, but he blamed them for Germany losing the Great War and for any shortcomings our country has had since. Johanna's family felt that hatred." She twists her hands together, but she meets my eye. "Within months of Hitler becoming chancellor, he declared a national boycott of Jewish businesses. Johanna's father was a doctor. Over time, his number of patients became fewer and fewer, until he had none. Johanna's family could barely put food on the table. I saw the change in her. Johanna was once so carefree, so quick to laugh. But then she was just . . . scared. Then she was gone. I miss her. She was my Marianne."

Four words that say so much.

So much history that I never saw through Johanna's eyes.

"I remember," I begin, not sure if my sister wants to talk about her more. But I go on, "I remember her. Not too well. But I remember how much you two laughed together."

One side of Angelika's mouth lifts in a sad smile. "I wish I could do something," she says, "to honor her."

"I know, my petunia," Papa says. "The time may come. But for now, we wait. We play our parts. Nothing can change. The pamphlets will keep coming. The White Rose mentioned forthcoming ones."

"How many?" I wonder out loud.

"My guess is they'll keep writing them until they're caught or until the war is finished. Pray the second one occurs first." Papa walks toward our wood-burning stove. Today's temperature is too warm for a fire, but he lights it and deposits the White Rose leaflet inside. He simply says, "For our safety."

Chapter 8

We play our parts. Papa's words echo in my mind long after he burns our leaflet to nothing more than ashes. *Nothing can change.*

I agree. Of course I agree. Because I'm relieved to keep going to my soccer games and to my hikes and to the other JM activities, including the meetings. Our recent ones may have been filled with tension, but our normal meetings are filled with laughter and singing and silly games and, most important, with Marianne.

I don't want to stop going to any of it.

Angelika likewise keeps busy with her normal routine of lectures and concerts. She's always home by Adolf Hitler's nine o'clock curfew.

All the while, I wonder when the next bombing will

come and if it'll be closer to home. I never have to wonder long. Seemingly every other day, England's air force bombs a city somewhere in Germany. The blessing—for us—is that Papa's imaginary circle hasn't grown any larger. All the recent attacks are up north, along the coast, where the air raids are still targeting docks, plants, seaports, and submarine yards.

I also wonder with more urgency when the next leaflet will come, and if poor Rita will suddenly vanish from our JM meetings like Adelita did.

To my relief, nearly two weeks pass, and I still see Rita's freckled face at school and at our meetings, even if she's hesitant to make eye contact with anyone at JM.

Then the fourth leaflet arrives. Papa doesn't hide it from me.

It begins with a proverb:

PAY ATTENTION OR PAY THE CONSEQUENCES. A SMART CHILD WILL ONLY BURN HIS FINGERS ONCE ON A HOT STOVE.

It says everything that comes out of Hitler's mouth is a lie.

WHEN HE SAYS PEACE, HE MEANS WAR.

It talks of senseless deaths. A lot of them. Too many of them.

At the end, they add two interesting things.

The first is a promise that they won't stop. The White Rose will be our guilty conscience.

The second is that the White Rose writers give a *reassurance*—their word, not mine—that the addresses were chosen at random from address books. And the addresses aren't documented in writing anywhere.

I want to believe it, but Rita's family did feel targeted, since the leaflet suggested posting it in beer halls. And when Elisabeth asks us who received the latest leaflet, all heads turn to look at poor Rita. I turn, too. I think it's my guilty conscience.

No one else will admit if their family has received the pamphlet.

I certainly don't.

And even while Papa, Angelika, and I let the White Rose's anti-Hitler words sink in, I know it won't rouse my family in the way they want it to. Papa still buys the official newspaper of the Nazi Party—and makes sure he's seen while doing so. I continue to collect donations for the army and mend Hitler Youth uniforms. Angelika will still go to Ulm in a few weeks to fulfill her service to Adolf Hitler.

We'll do it all, for Angelika's safety and so that Papa's true views won't be discovered. We'll do it all, turning a blind eye to others in need.

The White Rose said they weren't going to stop, but the weird thing is . . . days go by without Papa pulling a new leaflet from our mailbox. The first four pamphlets came within fifteen days. But my school year ends a week later. Angelika's semester concludes ten days after that.

Still, there's nothing.

It's for the best, I tell myself. I have bigger things to worry about, like Angelika leaving for a munitions plant while plants and factories are being bombed up north. Too soon, it's August and the time has come for my sister to board a train for Ulm.

Papa doesn't like it. Oh, he hates it.

"Hide it," he tells Angelika. He doesn't need to tell

her. Angelika knows she needs to appear 100 percent able-bodied. She knows she can't fall behind in her quota. But Papa needs to say it.

Angelika lets him.

On the train platform, our little family hugs. I wish Tigerlily were here. She's part of the family, too.

When the train whistle sounds, Papa squeezes us again. "Be careful, Angelika." He holds her hand through the train's window as long as humanly possible.

As the sound of the train fades, I touch his shoulder as he stands on the platform, staring at nothing but the empty track, his arms dangling at his sides. "She'll hide it," I reassure him. And because I know he's nervous about the war coming to Ulm, I also say, "All the bombings have been up north."

"You've been listening to my radio?" he asks me.

"I worry about her, too." I think of Papa's map, a new city marked almost every day, but not Frankfurt. Not yet. Still, I'm uneasy. "I worry about us, too."

"So do I," Papa says.

That night, there's a storm. There's thunder. The

rainfall is torrential. And the hailstones, pinging on the sidewalk outside my window, are the size of tennis balls.

I rub Tigerlily between her ears to settle her. I'd scratch her belly, but when I do that, she tends to get twitter-pated and playfully responds with her teeth. "I don't have thick fur like you," I always scold her excitement. Yet I'm the fool who keeps going near her tummy with my bare hands. No way I want her teeth near me on a night like this when she's excited in all the wrong ways. Milk, I decide, could help distract her from the cracking sky.

I head toward the kitchen but make it only a step outside my bedroom. Angelika's light is on. Strange, as Angelika is in Ulm. I go into her room, finding Papa on his hands and knees. He has a crowbar and he's currently prying up a length of Angelika's hardwood floor. Three long pieces are already removed.

"Papa?"

My voice is lost in a peal of thunder.

I try again. Papa startles. "Did you hear me working?" he asks.

"No," I say slowly, drawing out the word, a question in my voice. "What are you doing?"

"Using the storm to cover the noise."

That tells me little. I widen my eyes.

"I'm putting in a trapdoor."

I lean forward to better see beneath our floor. "Is that our building's cellar?"

Papa nods.

I'm confused. The door that leads to the shared basement is only two apartments down the hall; yet here he is tearing up the floor—of an apartment we don't even own—to give us direct access to the building's basement. "Are you allowed to do this?" I ask.

Papa's blue eyes are clear as day. "If there's a siren or any other type of threat, I want us to get below ground as quickly as possible, my cornflower."

The idea is sobering. A siren means bombs.

"What will the air siren sound like?" I ask Papa.

"Almost like a whooshing sound, as if the sound travels in a circular motion, getting farther and then looping closer."

I nod, shivering at the thought of it. Outside, thunder

booms. I jump. Papa reacts by yanking off another floor-board. The two cracks sound as one. "Need help?" I ask.

Tigerlily supervises by the door, mewing her dissatisfaction with the evening. When we're done—with a hole and the floorboards held together—the trapdoor is able to lift as a single piece. Angelika's rug is fashioned to the contraption, so when the door is flipped open and closed, the rug goes with it. As clever as Papa's invention is, and the fact that when the door is closed, the rug conceals it, I hope we'll never have to use it.

Chapter 9

Rita and I have one more street-block before we split ways on our walk home from school. She stops mid-sentence, her hand closing over my arm.

"What is it?" I ask.

But then I see.

Up ahead, just a block away, is a truck painted with the swastika of the Nazi Party. Men with guns leap from each door and storm a building. It looks like an apartment building.

We stop walking.

We can't help but watch.

The men wear normal clothes. Not uniforms. Many officers wear a gray-green tunic. Storm troopers, who are the Nazi Party's militia, wear brown uniforms.

They're sometimes called brownshirts. But these men aren't either of those things.

I realize that these men are Gestapo. They're part of Hitler's secret police, the ones who spy on Germany to identify anyone who opposes Hitler.

Inside the building, there's screaming. A child wails.

Rita grips my arm harder as a man and a woman are forced outside.

"Do you think it's about the leaflets?" Rita whispers. "Are they being arrested—"

"Shh, I don't know," I say, and I roughly swallow.

Others have stopped to watch as well. A man narrows his eyes. A woman covers her mouth. Another woman leads her child away. We should be going away, too.

But then a third person is removed from the building.

It's a girl, around our own age. She's kicking, screaming, crying. Her arms are pinned behind her back.

The word *Jew* is spat by the Gestapo man dragging her.

"They were hiding her," I manage to mumble.

"No," Rita says, but not in disagreement. She's stunned or frightened. Both.

I remember now that a Jewish children's home was shut down earlier this year. The kids who lived there were said to have been deported. Is this girl from that home? Did she not leave Germany?

I wish she had.

"We should go," I say, and turn away from the people being forced toward the truck. We need to distance ourselves from the chaos. Rita, gripping my arm, turns with me. My feet move, but my brain stays behind. It stays on the Jewish girl being taken away, on the two Aryan-looking people being arrested, on the sound of a screaming child still inside. Adelita bursts into my mind, and how that child will likely be placed with a new Nazi family like Adelita probably was.

I lean into Rita and talk into her ear. "Don't tell anyone what we saw."

"Why?"

I say under my breath, "They'll ask questions."

"But we did nothing wrong."

"I know, but it's better not to say anything. We could say the wrong thing. Lie," I add, "in the future, if your family gets any more leaflets."

"Brigitte?"

"Just do it."

I want to tell her that she's already come across as sympathetic, but the more I say, the more trouble I could get myself into.

Rita shudders. "This is the first time I've ever seen someone taken like that. Have you?"

I hesitate.

"You have," she says.

I shake my head. "No." I stop. I think it through. I suck in a deep breath of air, and then I close my mouth. Here I am again, wanting to say more. My heart is pounding from what we witnessed, and I want to say I've heard similar stories. I almost mention my neighbor. I almost reveal the full story about Adelita. That, yes, Adelita left suddenly, just as Elisabeth told us. But Adelita was taken. Adelita isn't likely to come back. She didn't take an impromptu trip like Elisabeth implied. Instead, Elisabeth lied.

But I hold those words in.

I have to.

I won't be the one to shatter Rita's hopes of being

reunited with her best friend. I won't be the reason why she cries for Adelita like my sister did for Johanna.

Then there's how I cautioned Rita to lie about the leaflets. I've already said too much. That warning could already get me—and my family—in enough hot water. I can only imagine what would happen if Elisabeth found out I was spreading so-called rumors about Adelita's disappearance. It's not something I want to imagine.

Adolf Hitler is scary.

His war is scary.

At the kitchen table, I rub my temples, barely tasting my breakfast. Papa has the radio on low, but I still hear the reports of a new city shelled with bombs. I wish I was canoeing on a lake with Marianne, but instead I take a bite of bread and slide today's newspaper toward me.

HATE IS OUR PRAYER—AND VICTORY OUR REWARD.

Before, I never made an effort to read the newspaper. But I want to now, even if the words are one-sided—the Nazi Party's side—and those words are today's front-page headline. I scrunch my nose at it because I'm confused how *hate* and *victory* go together.

The next pages of the newspaper list the death sentences of German people who oppose Adolf Hitler. I wonder what the rules are for being taken to a camp versus being taken to a prison versus being executed. Or if any rules exist. I wonder if Adelita's brother and Papa were named in a previous newsprint.

Here, it names a priest, along with a group of students. The students—one hundred and fifty-two of them, that number so exact I shudder—did nothing more than hang anti-Nazi posters. That's it. All of them were executed. All of them so close in age to Angelika.

I shake my head in sadness and disgust. Then I see it. A German man and woman who were hiding a young Jew—the people Rita and I saw get arrested. They have names. Kurt Becker. Frieda Becker. The young girl's name isn't listed.

Days have gone by and I'm still rattled by what I witnessed on the street. I told Papa, and he hugged me, muttering, "When will it all end?"

Papa left the *all* undefined. But I can't help thinking

it, and how we bomb England while they bomb us. How we fight on the ground in Russia. How Hitler ruthlessly targets a heritage different than his own. How he invades countries to grow our German numbers, yet he has no problem harming his own German citizens.

I turn the page of the newspaper as Papa stands from his radio. He rakes a hand through his hair as he leaves the room.

The back pages of the newspaper are devoted to obituaries of fallen soldiers, giving notice of their deaths.

It's all too much.

I close the newspaper, but my eyes betray me and fall on the headline again, about how victory is our reward. How are *any* of these deaths a victory? What will be left of Germany once Adolf Hitler wins?

It says here he is winning.

Papa comes back in with the mail. He flips from one piece to the next and I watch his expression. It'll sour if a leaflet is in his stack. But then his face lights up and I jump from my chair.

At once I recognize Angelika's handwriting, where

she exaggerates the crossing on her *t*, the line swooping through the entire word.

All is well, she writes. She's met a girl who also goes to her same university. The girl, Sophie, has become a fast friend. My sister calls her *a great companion to have by my side.*

And while Angelika is discreet in her letter, I can read between the lines that this Sophie has been helping make sure my sister meets her daily production quotas that Papa's been fretting about.

I wonder again whether, if Marianne knew about Angelika's long-term effects of polio, she would tell Elisabeth. Or, I think, what if I had a disability; would Marianne report me? But then I chastise myself for questioning her loyalty to me. Lately, I've kept so much from *her*. In the past, I would've whispered to her about how Papa secretly created a trapdoor in our apartment. Actually, I would've invited her over to see it firsthand, taking turns lowering each other through to get the full experience. But everything feels upside down right now. So I've kept that to myself. The omission makes me feel guilty, which doesn't seem fair because Marianne's always been there for me. Not for Adelita Vogel, I remind myself, but for me, yes.

In fact, I remember how she helped me during our Jungmädel Challenge during summer camp. Our leaders were fervent about how everyone in the Hitler Youth needed to be fit and healthy. There wasn't a single if, and, or but about passing the fitness tests that make up the Jungmädel Challenge. If you didn't pass, the rumor was you couldn't be part of our group anymore.

At first, the thought was unbearable. But then I used it as motivation. The sixty-meter run in twelve seconds wasn't a problem. I jumped well over the required two and a half meters. Marianne and I swam side by side for our one-hundred-meter loop. The challenge became fun. I enjoyed and excelled at the somersaulting and tightrope walking. But then came the two-hour march, nearly ten kilometers, in neat rows of coordinated girls, which I didn't realize would be a problem—until my ankle twisted in a rut, not even three kilometers in. A small yelp interrupted my singing. I kept walking, trying to keep up the even march, but my ankle hurt too much.

Marianne noticed and glanced down, before fixing her eyes straight ahead, like they were supposed to be.

"It's an out-and-back," Marianne told me, speaking from the corner of her mouth. The singing and drumbeat overpowered her voice so only I heard. "Slip out. Wait until we march back, then join us again."

My heart pounded as I agreed to the scheme. Frau Weber remained at the start and finish, but I was afraid one of the other girls would notice. I stepped aside, feigning that I was tying my boot. Marianne shifted a little to her left, marching for the both of us. On the way back, I joined our cavalry again, hoping the waving banners of the girls in front of me would shield me. Still, the girl behind me made a noise deep in her throat—like an ugly frog had taken up residence there—but Marianne spat over her shoulder, "She's hurt. But she'll be fine. It's not a big deal. Stop being a buttinski."

The girl looked offended, as if Marianne had slapped her. "It's not a big deal?" she snapped. "The Führer wants girls who are strong and able-bodied."

In that moment, it felt like a punch to my gut, more painful than the burn in my ankle. Because, while I had a temporary ankle sprain, my sister was in Switzerland at that very moment, trying to learn how to hide that she'd never be able-bodied again. Humiliation swept through me. For Angelika. For myself. I was the dolt who tripped. I was the girl who had the disabled sister who the Führer didn't want.

"Her ankle will be fine," Marianne insisted.

The girl turned up her nose. "You better hope so."

Back at camp, I had felt embarrassed. But now I feel ashamed. Ashamed because my sister had been doing everything within her power to hide herself from Hitler. And me . . . I'd been jumping through hoops to show my support for the same deplorable man.

A man who doesn't want my sister.

But you know what? Angelika doesn't want him either.

And neither do I.

Papa is smiling, happy to hear from Angelika's letter that she's well. During the summer recess, he's been practically glued to his radio, listening for anything that'd lead him to believe Ulm may become a target. Papa even has a bag by the door, with the exact fare it'd take for us to travel to Ulm to sweep up my sister and bring her home. By the trapdoor, we have what I've come to think of as our Bomb Bags, with extra clothing, necessities, and things that can't be replaced, like photos of Mama.

The image of Papa hunching over our radio, the fact he has a plan to save my sister, the mere existence of our Bomb Bags . . . it only adds to the newspaper headline and all the senseless deaths—and it makes me madder.

Papa's smile vanishes. "What is it, Brigitte?" His attention flicks to the letter, confused.

"It's Hitler," I say. "He's hurting so many people and he wants to hurt so many more. I see that now. You don't trust him. You don't support him. And I don't either. I don't either, Papa."

I'm in his arms then, Papa's chin on the top of my head. "I won't let Hitler or his war have you or your sister," Papa says.

"Or you," I add.

"Or me," he whispers. "We'll be fine. We'll stay together."

Papa's words are soothing. His arms around me are a haven. But my nose prickles with emotions for the hundreds of thousands of people who Hitler has hurt too badly for my mind to ever fully comprehend.

Chapter 10

Hitler and his war . . . it continues to be smothering, each hour, each day, and each week that goes by. It doesn't matter that the fighting is far away on Russian soil or along our northern coastline.

But then that distance changes, and I know the exact instant it does because Papa grabs his radio with both his hands and shakes it, as if he can alter what the broadcast is saying.

But he can't, and what it says is that Frankfurt has been bombed.

Frankfurt.

Before, Papa said, "I don't see München getting hit before Frankfurt. When there's news of Frankfurt, then . . ." and he trailed off, and now . . . Frankfurt has news.

I've worried over it, I've dreaded it, and now it's happened: Papa's imaginary circle has grown.

From our living room, I watch the sky. It's the same blue sky. I see birds, not planes. I hear other kids in the street. A trolley car passes.

From where Papa sits, listening to the radio, he doesn't look out the window, but he keeps glancing at his bag by the door. I sit across from him, hands clenched in my lap. I shift my eyes to the strip of row homes and apartments across from ours. I can't imagine seeing them as rubble. But as I stare, I expect to hear a siren any moment now. I expect the planes to scare the birds away.

But the day goes on. Days go on, in fact.

When school begins again, Papa walks me there. When it's time for lunch, he walks me home. When lunch is over, he walks me back to school. When I leave school, there he is. I wonder if he ever left. The fact the flower bed next to the school's entrance has been weeded makes me think Papa didn't go anywhere.

"You waited this whole time?" I ask. My eyes flick to the sky.

"Did not," he says.

I raise a brow, questioning his honesty.

He snorts. "I went home"—he pauses—"to get the mail, then I came back."

My next raised brow means something entirely different.

"Nothing from *them*," he says. "But our petunia sent us another letter."

I nearly dive into his coat pocket to find the letter. Papa laughs, retrieving it for me.

Angelika's well, as well as she can be while standing over a machine sixty hours a week, going through the same motion again and again, to make guns. The Russian women have it worse, though, she says. With our troops invading their lands, the women are taken as prisoners and are forced to work at our factories. And not just for sixty hours, but for seventy, maybe longer, with only watery soup in their bellies. At night, the Russian women sleep in barracks behind barbed wire.

Angelika thinks the way the women are treated is cruel.

Papa says, "She puts too much in her letters."

Maybe so, but: "Is it a good sign we have all those Russian prisoners?" I ask hesitantly. It feels mean to call them prisoners, as if I'm back in medieval times. But here we are, in the 1940s, and Germany has prisoners. And I can't grasp how invading other countries and taking these women will make Germany better. How will any of this make Germany any better?

Papa says, "I don't know, Brigitte. Of course Angelika is right: It is cruel to these women. But I don't know what it means for the war. All we can do is wait."

We'll wait to see if Hitler will win. If a bomb will strike here. Or if it'll strike Ulm.

What happens is that bombs are dropped on Frankfurt a second time.

Then only a few days later, a bombing in the north damages two factories, hospitals, and schools.

Schools.

My belly has so many butterflies I worry my feet will leave the ground, taking me right into the sky with England's planes. At least from that height I'd know what they are doing. Right now, England's bombs are a mystery. They struck Frankfurt twice. But the strike on the schools and hospitals was along the coast again. They bombed Augsburg, so close to us and to Ulm, but that was nearly six months ago.

Papa waits for me again after school. That day at school, we practiced running to a shelter. Papa saw Rita and me go by. Now he gives me a tight smile. Rita, too. Papa walks us straight to our JM meeting. Along the way, we don't say much. Truth be told, Rita hasn't been as talkative with me after I told her to keep quiet about what we saw, as if I asked her to be part of a conspiracy, when I was only trying to protect her.

Before I go inside the clubhouse, I look at Papa. After my declaration to him in the kitchen, I don't want to go in and pretend to be the perfect Nazi. But Papa nods for me to do just that.

He's already sitting on the steps before I'm inside the door.

Marianne greets me with a hug. When she pulls back, she says, "I see your papa outside still."

On impulse, I say, "He built a trapdoor in our apartment."

"He did what?"

I let out a big breath of air. It feels good to tell my best friend that. Then I laugh. A bombing is a serious thing. Marianne's comical expression, however, is not. "In Angelika's floor, Papa made a hole so we can jump down to the building's cellar. It's hidden by a rug."

"But why?" Marianne's smile wanes. And I remember how Angelika mentioned trapdoors being used to hide Jews.

I spit out, "In case the siren goes off."

Marianne nods, and relief floods me.

"We have to go all the way down the street to a shelter," she says. "So that's smart, if you ask me. But was he allowed to do that?"

"Nope. And I helped."

Marianne laughs at that. "And you used a rug to hide it?"

"Yes, the rug is attached to the door. You'd never know the door was there, unless you, well, knew already."

My best friend swings her arm around my shoulder and says, "Brigitte Annette Schmidt, I never knew you were such a lawbreaker, vandalizing private property like that."

"That's me," I say. Hearing my full name—Brigitte Annette Schmidt—fills me with warmth. My middle name is for my mama, in remembrance. And now I remember how she was a lawbreaker the day she met Papa. I like that I have some Annette in me.

"Don't tell anyone, though, about the trapdoor," I say to her. "I don't want my papa to get in any trouble."

"I won't," Marianne says. "Promise."

Chapter 11

I'm startled awake. An alarm is going off. I listen for—one, two, three, four, five—seconds as it seems like the deep noise is getting farther and farther away, then it's as if the sound loops back and is coming closer again, becoming more high-pitched.

My breath hitches at the exact moment that Papa barrels into my room. I know what's happening.

München is about to be bombed.

England is on their way here.

But how far away are they?

Close enough, I guess, for the air raid siren to go off and for Papa to hurry me out of bed. My arms quake as I push myself to my feet and hold Tigerlily to my chest. Papa takes a robe from the bottom of my bed. "Here, my cornflower. Move quickly."

Tigerlily's claws dig into my stomach.

Papa takes her from me. As one arm, then another goes into my robe, I expect Papa to put our cat down. I've never seen him hold her before. Papa likes Tigerlily, but Tigerlily was Mama's, until she became mine.

Papa cradles Tigerlily with one arm, shaking out my school rucksack with the other. Tigerlily goes inside. Papa jostles the zipper, pulling my bag closed as my cat tries to poke her head out. Once done, Papa hands Tigerlily back to me.

Robe on, my cat in a bag in my arms, the siren blaring around us, Papa says, "Let's go."

I hesitate, everything about this moment feeling bizarre. Though it's not as if a bomb hitting München was unlikely. I saw Papa's map. I grew his imaginary circle in my head. But I never could bring myself to see my city as rubble. Or the skies a ghostly pink from flames.

"Brigitte!"

I stumble forward toward my sister's room, finding an odd comfort in the fact that Tigerlily's claws still pierce through my bag and into my skin. Everything unfolding around me feels surreal, so dreamlike. But those sharp nails on all eighteen of her toes are keeping me tethered to the here and now. Papa already has the door open and the rug flipped over. His arms are outstretched, waiting for me.

Next thing I know, my feet hit the hard ground of the cellar.

It's dark.

I squeeze Tigerlily within my rucksack even closer.

My Bomb Bag lands, then Papa's.

Then Papa is beside me.

It's darker, the door having closed as Papa lowered himself.

His footsteps bound.

A light bulb flicks on when Papa pulls its string.

He pulls another.

My heart and breath pound the entire time.

No one else is in the cellar with us. We're the first to make it below ground. There's only random boxes and suitcases and some nonperishable food that people from the building have started to store here in our communal shelter.

Papa's contraption quickened our ability to get here, where we're safe. Or as safe as we can be while planes drop bombs on whatever is aboveground.

Though—

"I don't hear any bombs," I whisper to Papa.

"No," he says, crouching, unable to stand at his full height. "Not yet." He cranes his head back to peer at the ceiling as if he can see through into Angelika's room and through the other three floors on top of ours and into the night sky.

That's when the ground shakes.

I no longer wonder how far away the English are. They are *here*.

The cellar's regular door—not our secret, private entrance—flies open and a man stumbles in, as much from his haste as from the shock of the first bomb hitting München.

Without looking at me, Papa blindly pushes the top of my head, until I'm sitting on the ground. His eyes never leave the ceiling until our neighbor calls his name.

They meet, speaking in hushed voices.

The ground shakes again. I hear muffled booms.

More people enter. Parents rush their children to sit by me, knees pulled to their chests. I know some of them, from school, from hellos in the lobby, from seeing them around. We exchange timid smiles. But we're all too nervous to talk. The grown-ups do the talking, but away from us.

Another muffled boom. And another. Tigerlily mews.

I unzip my rucksack enough for Tigerlily's head to escape and I whisper "Shh" to her over and over. When I close my eyes and rub my face against her fur, I picture Marianne and her family running down the street, through the bursts of light in the night, toward a shelter. *Please let them make it.*

The siren stops. We're past warnings.

The little boy next to me doesn't blink as he stares at my cat's orange-and-white-striped head. "You can pet her," I say.

So he does, for what seems like hours.

The entire time, bombs whistle and boom over our heads, shaking the concrete ground, releasing dust and dirt from the cellar's beams.

The light bulbs flicker, but they stay on.

I meet Papa's gaze as he watches one of the bulbs. Then he crosses the room to me. He sits and holds me to him, speaking only to me. "The bombs are hitting another part of the city. If they were striking here, we'd feel it more. The lights wouldn't stay on."

I nod, beginning to shiver from the cellar's damp ground, the night cool. "Do you think that Ulm—"

"I don't know." Papa licks his lips. "Time will tell. But let's hope they've only come here tonight and that your sister is safe."

For the rest of the night and into the morning, I huddle next to Papa and stare at the bulb closest to me, praying for it to stay on. Wherever Marianne is, I pray for her light to be on, too. In Ulm, I hope that my sister is sleeping soundly through the night.

Chapter 12

In the morning, or what I assume to be morning in this windowless room, the cellar lights still work. The muffled booms have stopped. At some point, I fell asleep. I blink my eyes. I'm propped against Papa, who leans against the cinderblock wall. Tigerlily is free from my rucksack and curled on Papa's lap.

All my neighbors still seem to be here, most of them sleeping. Frau Roth and her husband converse softly. Papa wakes and begins talking with the others, a sponge for anything he can find out. But everyone has been trapped here the entire night.

My throat's dry, my neck is stiff, there's a layer of ceiling debris all over my robe, and I have to use the bathroom. But the walls still stand around me. I own more than what's in my Bomb Bag.

What will we find outside?

I want to go. I have to see.

We return to our apartment through the real exit and walk the hallway until our door. Inside, I put Tigerlily down and she scurries toward our bedroom and what she knows. The apartment looks exactly how we left it, with Papa's plants everywhere and dishes in the sink that I put off until the morning. But everything feels different, like if I breathe too deeply, it'll all come tumbling apart.

As soon as Papa and I change from our pajamas, we go outside. The air is chilly and I sink deeper into my coat, wanting to also escape the smell of chemicals and ash in the air. Above me, the sky is full of sunlight, and that's something. Planes only come under the cover of night. But that ash is coming from somewhere.

A siren goes off, not the whooping of the air raid siren but the screech of an emergency vehicle. With so many overlapping sounds, there must be multiple fire and police vehicles.

Papa grips my hand. We leave our neighborhood and pass Papa's university. It's untouched. The park is still the park. Many others move in our same direction—all of them curious about their businesses, about the destruction, desperate to find their loved ones. The sky isn't blue now, but dark from smoke. I don't see a single bird.

I pray again for Marianne.

I accept the fact, a few blocks later, that we're walking in the direction of her neighborhood.

A few blocks more and my feet have never felt heavier.

It *is* her neighborhood that was bombed.

It's on fire, and smoke curls away from the streets to sting my eyes. But I can't look away. In some places, a building is missing a wall and in others, there's no longer a building at all. Men run everywhere, calling out in case anyone trapped can hear them. I watch as two men groan to lift a beam, freeing an older woman beneath. They then grunt and soothe her as they carry her in their arms toward a makeshift medical tent.

They go back to search for more survivors.

Every one of my swallows is forced down. Papa's hand has never been tighter around mine. His eyes are wide, his head slowly turning, and we stand there. We simply stand there, at the onset of Marianne's neighborhood. People brush by us. A dog barks.

I croak out her name.

All Papa says is that we'll find her.

I see Marianne's disheveled braids first. She is deep within the assembly room of her school, surrounded by her mama and siblings, who are surrounded by hundreds of other people who are now without a home.

When we reach them through the crowd, I fling my arms around her. She's crying. No words, just tears. Papa goes to her mama, who he knows, but not overly well. They've mostly exchanged smiles and hellos at various events, drop-offs, pickups. One of Marianne's sisters is asleep in their mama's lap, her hand clasping her twin's, who's sleeping on a cot. Papa and Marianne's mama talk quietly.

I'm not sure what to say to Marianne, so I let her softly cry into my shoulder. She eventually says, "Our home is gone. We made it to the shelter in time. But this morning, we saw . . . it's gone."

I have no words. My home looks exactly the same. Hers no longer exists. I hug her tight.

I feel Papa standing over us. Then he says, "Girls, we should go."

Girls? As in plural girls? Not just me? Papa smiles weakly. "Marianne, we'd like you to stay with us for a while."

She looks to her mama, who says, "Yes, I think that'd be best. Your brother and sisters and I will go to your uncle's across town. But space will be cramped as it is. You'll do better at the Schmidts'. You and Brigitte have your meetings and events and . . ." Her mama trails off, her voice losing enthusiasm. "Soon your papa will be back from the war. I'll find us a new home by then."

Marianne's eyes are filled with tears, but she nods. I squeeze her hand and say, "You'll have your own room until Angelika is back in the next week or two."

She forces a smile, but after we get home, both of us walking like zombies from exhaustion, she asks if it'd be okay if she stayed with me in my room.

We sleep the rest of the day in my tiny bed.

When I wake, it's dark. Marianne stirs, too. We lie

there, side by side, not speaking, but I know we're both thinking the same thing . . . will the bombers be back?

Frankfurt was hit twice.

I remember another town getting hit three nights in a row.

There's this other city up north that's been hit at least ten times.

Could my neighborhood be next?

Chapter 13

Marianne is standing with her toes at the edge of the rug covering the trapdoor when I find her in the morning. I spent much of the night staring into the darkness, waiting for the sound of the air raid siren, until I finally fell back asleep. "It's nice your shelter is right beneath you," she says without turning to face me.

"Yes," I say softly.

"It was terrifying running down the street with those sirens blaring." Her voice is quiet but steady. "Anke tripped. In the moments it took Mama to get her back to her feet, Astrid nearly lost her mind. Don't ever try to separate twins. But we made it. All seven of us."

"I'm sorry."

She faces me. "Thanks for letting me stay with you

while"—she gestures in a wave—"my mama figures everything out."

I take her hand. "Come on, let's get something to eat."

Papa isn't home, but he left a note that he'd be back soon. I search the fridge for something easy. And, well, for something in general. Because of the war, food rationing is in full force. Papa and I are both allowed one egg every week. I hope Papa doesn't mind I give his to Marianne.

After we eat, Marianne picks at a loose thread in our tablecloth. "I haven't been here in a while," she says. "I forgot about the million plants your family has. Smells good."

I breathe in deeply, inhaling the lavender and peppermint that Papa keeps near the sink. She's right. My eyes fall on the nearby drawer. "Cards?" I ask.

She smiles. "Sure."

I retrieve the cards and start dealing the first game that comes to me: Tod und Leben.

I give Marianne the red cards. I keep the black ones.

Without me having to explain more, she knows

what game it is. War. Battle. Life or Death. It has various names.

We've played it so many times before at the JM clubhouse, or while waiting for a streetcar, or under a tree at the park.

She flips her first card. It's a four.

Before I reveal mine, I silently wish for it to be lower than hers. Marianne needs a win. I hide my smile when my card's a two.

She takes both our cards and adds them to her pile.

I win the next round and feign excitement.

We don't speak.

We just play.

Until we need to speak; we both play a ten. "War," we say in unison, which then produces matching giggles.

We both play another card facedown, before playing a faceup card to see who's won the battle.

I do.

Marianne sighs. "I'm tired of war."

"If you want, we can play a different—"

"I just want my papa to come home."

Oh. "He will, soon."

"The Führer needs to win first. Why can't he just win already?"

I swallow. I'm not sure how to answer that. Knowing what I now know—and I'm certain there's still plenty I don't know—I'm not sure I want Hitler to win. But if he loses, Germany loses. And Germany is my home.

What I do wish for is that I could simply freeze everyone involved. Hitler would stop invading other countries. The Russians would stop fighting us. Hitler would stop dropping bombs. England would stop attacking us. We'd all go our separate ways.

Hitler would be gone. Perhaps we can send him to Mars, where he's no longer our leader and where he doesn't have the power to hurt people like Johanna, and tear apart families like the Vogels simply because they believe differently than him, and sterilize people similar to Angelika, a so-called inconvenience to our country because of disabilities they have no control over.

Yes, Hitler needs to go to Mars. Or any other planet. Any planet but ours.

I wouldn't dare say it out loud, not in front of Marianne. I can't tell her I'm against Hitler now.

I wonder, though, if she forgets that Hitler drafted her papa to fight in the war. I wonder if she only wants Hitler to win so her papa can come home. Or does she still see Adolf Hitler as our Führer?

I rub my brow, my head suddenly hurting, and play another card.

Marianne's quick to play hers. I watch her and I feel a distance growing between us; maybe it's been growing for a while. I never told her about my family receiving the leaflets, after all. Then my breath hitches, because what if one arrives here while she's staying with us? Would she dare tell Elisabeth or Frau Weber that the White Rose sent us their anti-Nazi papers? Simply possessing a leaflet could have you arrested. Marianne said as much herself.

Papa's key jingles in the lock then, and I'm happy for the diversion.

"You're both finally up," he says in greeting. He drops the mail on the table. Papa wouldn't have been so cavalier if there'd been anything . . . dodgy . . . in that pile. Say, a new leaflet.

"Any news of Ulm?" I ask.

Papa says, "It wasn't bombed. Only München."

I'm relieved for my sister. Marianne rubs her thumb down the half deck of cards in her hands. I don't want to be having this conversation in front of her, but here she is. It's not lost on me that Papa endlessly listened to the radio in fear that Ulm would be hit. Yet it was our city that was targeted. This time at least. I have to ask, "Do you think they'll be back?"

Marianne's hands go still.

"I can't say for sure. But we're prepared. And so is your family, Marianne. Your uncle's building has a basement. Your mama told me."

She nods weakly.

I lay another card.

Our game goes on.

Later that night, Marianne asks if she can sleep in Angelika's room. My guess is so that she's closer to the trapdoor. I offer to sleep there, too, but she wants to be alone.

"Good night, then," I say.

Instead of returning the sentiment, Marianne bends and retrieves something at the leg of Angelika's bed. "Why does your sister have canned goods in here?"

"Good question," I say slowly. A question I know the answer to. Angelika uses the cans during her physical therapy, to help strengthen her left side. "I, um . . ." I begin. "I must've gotten distracted while putting the groceries away and carried the cans in here."

"And you put them beneath her bed?"

"Maybe they rolled under?" I suggest. "Or maybe Tigerlily did it. You know she's always up to something."

Marianne smiles at that. She hands the cans to me. "Well, good thing I saw them. They're expired, you know?"

Probably because my sister has been using these cans for years. "Huh," I say. "I'll have to be more careful."

And I mean it, about anything related to Angelika's disability. I scan the room for anything else that Marianne could find strange. She yawns.

"You're tired. Good night," I say quickly. This time she says it back, and I skedaddle out of there.

I'm tired, too, but I spend much of the night awake again. No bombs fall. On us, at least. In the morning, I find Papa by the radio. Three cities up north were bombed.

How horrible of me, but I'm glad they're far, far away again.

The damage to our city seems bad enough. People are still being recovered from beneath fallen beams and rubble.

Of course, Papa relays this to me in whispers while Marianne's in the bathroom. He won't let us leave the apartment, too afraid of the uptick in violence and looting. When Marianne phones her mama, she agrees for us to stay indoors.

That leaves us with a lot of time for board games and puzzles. We eventually pull out Juden Raus!, and she and I take turns rolling the dice and moving our "Jews" across the map toward "collection points" for removal. I never realized how sickening this game is until now.

"Shall we play with Papa's trains?" I ask.

Marianne only shrugs her agreement. We lay the tracks all through Papa's plants. Tigerlily particularly likes the train, and we laugh at her chasing it. Otherwise we don't talk too much. Frankly I'm nervous about us talking about *real* topics. I'm afraid I won't respond correctly to something Marianne says about Hitler, and she'll know I don't like him anymore. And I'm uncomfortable talking about what's going on outside, knowing her entire life has been uprooted.

She does say, "My mama's looked at one apartment already, but she thinks it's too small. I'd have to share with the twins and maybe even another of my sisters."

I make a face at that.

"I know," she says.

"Well, in the meantime, you have your own room here until Angelika comes home."

I mean it as a good thing, but Marianne's smile turns down.

After a week, schools reopen and we're both allowed to go. I can't wait to get outside. Marianne and I go our separate ways and I feel like I can breathe easier.

After school, we meet up again at a JM meeting.

Marianne is bombarded with hugs. So are two other girls who live in her same neighborhood.

"I'm so glad the three of you are safe," Elisabeth says. Then while she's talking to all of them, I sense her focus is on Marianne as she says, "You girls are on track to be leaders. We're going to pick up our volunteer efforts, too, so there'll be more ways to prove yourself."

Marianne practically grows two inches. "I won't let you down. I'll do anything I can to help win this war."

Elisabeth beams.

When Marianne glances at me, I have to force a smile. "Me too," I say. "I want Marianne's papa to come home soon."

"We all do," Elisabeth says warmly. "Let's meet tomorrow after school. We'll start planning then."

Everyone around me is devoted to Hitler. Or at least they act like they are. Like I do. What would my best friend think if she knew it was Hitler who I wanted to be stopped?

Chapter 14

Our small family spins around the kitchen, Papa's arms around both my sister and me. Annoyed with the commotion, Tigerlily leaps from the table. When she lands, a meow squeaks out of her, then she dashes from the room.

Angelika is home.

Papa has tears in his eyes.

I'm hopping from foot to foot like I have to pee. I was supposed to be at the clubhouse with Marianne, helping Elisabeth. But I weaseled my way out of it, catching Marianne before she went inside and telling her I had too much homework. She was disappointed I couldn't help, too. But I'm extra glad I told the white lie, considering Angelika surprised us by coming home today. All we knew was that it'd be a day in October.

But here she is, all in one piece. Maybe a little thinner, but Angelika has made it home safe and sound. And I'm excited to hear all about her time in Ulm.

Finally the three of us settle around the table, keeping the pot on the stove warm for Marianne. Papa goes on about how he's so glad to have Angelika home to assist with my cooking. Leave it to me to somehow make Irish stew, which is a soup, taste dry.

We all know he's glad for more than help with my cooking, though.

"Sophie was a lifesaver," Angelika says of her new friend from Ulm. "Halfway through each day, my hip started aching and my hand tired, but she'd pass off her work as mine. Not once did they look twice at me."

Papa smiles. "I like this Sophie."

"Good," Angelika says. "She's taking one of your courses this semester."

"The A is already hers."

My sister grins. Papa grins. We're all grinning, despite my soup. I like that my family is as whole as we can be, around our table, when there's so much uncertainty out there.

"Sophie was so kind in general," my sister says. She blows on her stew. "The other women . . . the Russian ones . . . they looked so scared. They couldn't speak our language, but Sophie gestured and smiled. She really managed to communicate with them."

"She sounds like a nice girl," I say, watching Angelika's face. A smile hasn't left it. She scoops her soup.

"Sophie really is. She cares about people. She's from Ulm, not far from the church we saw, the one with the tallest spire. There's this bridge nearby. Someone painted JEWS NOT DESIRABLE IN ULM on it. I saw how Sophie looked at the words, and that's when I knew we were like-minded. She even had her own Johanna who was taken away."

I ask, "The same name even?"

"No." She sips from her spoon. "But just that she lost her best friend, too. It was nice to be able to talk to her about it. About a lot of things, really. The last person who I felt understood me like Sophie does was Johanna. It felt good to be able to open up."

That part stings a bit, that Angelika waited four

years to be open like that—when I've been here the entire time. Though I guess I was too young and then my sister didn't know if she could fully trust me until recently. I fill my spoon, tilt the broth free, then scoop again. This time I eat it, refocusing on this moment as a happy one.

"I'm glad you have a new friend," Papa says.

"Me too," my sister says. "I feel bad for her, though. Her papa's in prison."

My eyes jump to our papa, the fear of him being taken still fresh in my mind. "What did he do?" I ask.

"Made the mistake of making some critical remark about Hitler to one of his employees. He owns a business. You'd think you could trust someone who works for you, but that employee ratted him out. Sophie's relieved it was only prison instead of a camp. He'll come home."

"Eyes and ears," Papa mumbles.

She repeats, "Eyes and ears."

"Eyes and ears," I say.

And Angelika cocks her head at me. She's been talking freely in front of me, but she hasn't heard me say it.

"I'm against Hitler, too. Just like you and Papa," I tell her.

At that moment, as if Hitler planned it himself, Marianne is putting her key into the door.

Our voices quiet as we wait for her.

We won't speak about Hitler anymore.

We each take a spoonful of stew.

Marianne enters the kitchen, then hesitates, seeing that Angelika is home, as if she'd walked into a private moment. She did. But she's important, too. "Look who surprised us," I say with a smile. Then I say, "There's stew on the stove for you."

"But it's not very good," Angelika says with a smirk.

I shake my head, biting back my own smile. "Come join us."

Marianne smiles, too, but it doesn't feel real. "Sure, let me just go get washed up. I'm glad you're home, Angelika."

Marianne goes into Angelika's room, where she's been staying the past few weeks, and I hear her gathering her things.

"Excuse me," I say, then I hurry toward the bedrooms.

Marianne has her bag together. I reach for it. "Here, let's move this into my room."

I get her settled there, then Marianne continues on to the washroom, and I'm eager to get back to the kitchen. There, Papa and Angelika are mid-conversation. Angelika is laughing. It's nice to hear her laugh.

Papa asks, "Does she have a big family?"

"Five kids, including her." Angelika looks at me. "We're talking about Sophie," she says. "Then there's her mama and papa. Her older brother, Hans, goes to the university, too. He's in a student group where he does half a year in the classroom and the other half with the military."

"Ah, a medic," Papa says.

Angelika nods. "He's in Russia now. So is her younger brother. He's in the military, too."

Papa jokes, "Two brothers. So the house isn't entirely made up of girls? Imagine that."

Tigerlily takes that moment to prance back into the room, her belly swaying from side to side, adding one more girl to the mix.

Angelika says, "I'm pretty sure their dog is a boy, too."

I smile at Papa's exaggerated groan. Even growing up, Papa had a sister on either side of him. We know he loves his girls, Mama included, and I hold my breath a moment, wondering if he'll start hiccuping stories about her again. But then I think, no, he won't talk about Mama right now, because even if his outside is smiling, his insides could be remembering my brothers or sisters Mama lost in her belly between Angelika and me. And then it'll pummel me, like it always does, realizing I'm the baby who was born, but at the cost of Mama.

But then Marianne joins us, and the moment passes, and our conversation turns to school, and food, and finally being reunited.

By the end of November, Angelika is back at the university, Papa is back teaching, Marianne and I are busy with school and our JM activities, and we all fall into a routine. Routine is good, a way to keep my mind off the war.

During the day, it's easier, but at night, that's when I stare at the ceiling and expect to hear the siren whooping. I wonder if Marianne does, too, across the room on the cot Papa got her. But it's too dark to ever tell if her eyes are open.

To our surprise, there haven't been any more bombings. And I mean . . . anywhere. Since September, the air's been miraculously quiet throughout Germany.

I won't say this to Marianne, but I can't help thinking that Hitler so badly wants a victory in Russia—where her papa is fighting—that he's pushing with everything he's got there. It all makes me want to scream. But I don't even know *what* I'd scream. Not when I don't want Hitler to win, but I also don't want Germany to lose. If we lose, it could be at the cost of people like Marianne's papa, or the brothers of Angelika's new friend Sophie.

One day, Angelika comes home with her hair shorter. It looks nice, but different. Before, it was long enough to wear in braids. Now it bounces around her face, highlighting her sharp cheekbones and pretty eyes. Instead of reacting to my sister, Papa looks at me. "Please don't cut off your braids as well. You're both getting too old."

Angelika's newly nineteen. I'll be thirteen soon. Well, in four months.

Angelika also starts going out more, too, to study groups and such. One night, she nearly skids into the apartment right before Hitler's curfew, and Marianne and I look up from our homework.

From where I'm sitting, I can see the door. Thankfully, farther down the table, Marianne cannot.

Angelika is breathless. She practically leans on the door after she closes it and all her weight is on her good side.

Marianne starts to giggle. "Barely made it, Angelika!" she calls.

I giggle, too, but my laughter is forced and a large part of me worries about Angelika's hurrying.

"But I made it," Angelika calls back, still breathless.

Marianne laughs at that, too.

I study my sister's every movement as she heads toward her bedroom. She's not as in control of her hobbling as she usually is, but at least she's not using the wall for support. I widen my eyes at her as she passes.

“I’m fine,” she whispers. I flick my eyes to Marianne, but she’s focused on her homework again.

Frau Roth already questioned me about my sister’s limp, but I was luckily able to talk my way out of it. Now Angelika is being needlessly careless. What if Marianne notices? I’m not saying my best friend would tell Elisabeth. I’m not saying I know Marianne’s exact reaction either.

For the week that Marianne goes to her uncle’s to be with her family for the holidays, it’s a nice break from those back and forth unknowns and we can talk freely at suppertime again. Angelika goes on endlessly about Sophie.

Sophie likes to draw and paint and read.

She was once a kindergarten teacher.

Sophie enjoys music.

She has a lot of friends, and those friends are becoming my sister’s friends. Angelika has never had a group of friends like this before.

Angelika says, “They make me laugh, especially Sophie.” Like Johanna once did. The thought is a balm on my uneasiness that Angelika hasn’t been as careful lately with her new friends. She adds, "A bunch of us are going to the speech tomorrow at the university."

"I should probably listen in," Papa says in a disinterested voice.

I say, "My JM group will be there. We're collecting donations."

After supper, Marianne returns from her week away.

In the morning, we head toward the university. The speech is in honor of the university's founding 470 years ago. I wonder if the weather was as biting then as it is now. It's the coldest day in January yet, and my breath puffs out above my scarf and beneath my hat. With our long JM overcoats, Marianne and I look like brown mummies.

More and more people are arriving in the square and along the boulevard. Elisabeth and Marianne decided it'd be the perfect time to ask for donations for the war. I extend my cup to a group of people. "For the war efforts," I say simply. I smile. I wait, my arm out, my cup turned toward them. Within the group of five, two people drop in Reichsmarks. The coins clang against the bottom of my cup.

I hope Marianne is having more success. It's likely, since her heart is in it. Mine isn't. I'm only here because Papa wants everyone to believe we're good little Nazis.

The assembly begins and a man takes the temporary stage.

I listen, but not entirely. I feel the cold more than I hear his words.

The other JM girls are spread out through the crowd. Papa and Angelika are around here somewhere, too.

The man talking has an angry tone to his voice. Odd, as this is a celebration. Or so I thought. The people I approach next wear confused expressions, too, one girl fully scowling. I don't ask them for donations after all.

I search the crowd for Marianne. It's hard, with all of us bundled up, but I find her and ask, "Who's the man talking?"

"Seriously?" she says. "It's Herr Giesler. Our governor. A high-ranking Nazi official. My goodness, Brigitte, you're lucky Elisabeth didn't hear you ask that."

I ignore that and say, "What's he saying? Some people look upset."

Marianne shakes her head. "It's because it's mostly

students here and he's saying that they're too busy with their noses in books while the war is going on. He says they're using their studies to dodge the draft."

"He's actually saying that?"

"Of course he is."

I listen now.

"Falsely clever minds," he says, "are not an expression of real life. Real life is transmitted to us only by Adolf Hitler, with his light, joyful, life-affirming teachings!"

I'm not sure what that means. But some people boo and hiss under their breaths.

Their responses only worsen as Herr Giesler continues speaking about Hitler and how unimportant their studies are, and now the voices grow louder and louder, especially when he turns his attention from the male students to the female ones.

A girl shouts, "I can do more than produce babies!"

Those nearby cheer at what she says.

But what Herr Giesler is saying is the exact opposite. He's saying that all these girls are wasting their time at the university, when they should be with their husbands, using their healthy bodies and presenting the Führer with babies.

He uses those exact words: presenting the Führer with babies.

Never before have I wondered about what I'll be when I grow up. I haven't because I've been taught my whole life that my role is to be a future mother of Germany to ensure the Reich exists for the next thousand years. But now my mouth drops open at realizing how wrong it sounds that someone is telling me that a mother is all I can and should want to be. The angry girls and women around me assert that they can be something else, if they choose. And I realize that I want the choice, too.

"Ridiculous," Marianne says into my ear. "Can you believe these people?"

I can. I eye the crowd, seeing the faces of one student after another who doesn't agree with what's being spoken. There are also the faces of those who agree with what Herr Giesler shouts into the microphone.

Like Marianne's. "They'll all be arrested," she says with disgust in her voice. "What fools."

I search for Papa, but I can't find him. There are too many people. Hundreds of them. One student near me announces he's leaving. He gets to his feet. Heads turn toward him. That one student . . . that one student is all it takes to incite the crowd. Others begin to stand.

Marianne gasps. I follow her gaze to see two older boys fighting, dodging each other's fists. I look again to the stage, hoping that Herr Giesler will stop his tirade. Why is he still talking after so many people have gotten upset?

A man's voice shouts. I jump at the new sound and see he's a storm trooper, based on his brown suit, separating the two fighting boys. Another storm trooper helps him, and the boys are swiftly put in handcuffs.

More people are on their feet. More fights break out. More storm troopers swarm the crowd. Marianne is knocked to the ground, the coins from her cup scattering among the shoes that surround her. I quickly help her up and we run to the edge of a fountain. We climb onto its ledge as I sidestep a stray elbow. With the fountain emptied of water for the winter, I step into it, and then pull Marianne in, too. There we stand, huddled together, watching the chaos around us that only took seconds to brew, the shouting and scuffling rising in volume.

I realize I dropped my donation cup at some point.

I look for Papa again. I scan for Angelika. I spot Rita, running away from the crowd with another girl from our group.

In the boulevard, men and women are linking arms, creating a chain of three or four people. Another chain walks behind them. They march, shouting and singing.

Their words are against the Reich and against Hitler.

My breath comes out as quick puffs. Then my breath hitches. There, walking arm in arm with the others down the boulevard, her mouth wide-open as she protests, is my sister.

Chapter 15

Angelika?

I tell myself I'm wrong. The square and the boulevard are a sea of people, hundreds of bodies—marching, fleeing, fighting, falling, jostling, shouting. But there she is, her arm linked with another girl's, and together they walk with purpose down the road with an older boy and third girl as if they're part of a parade.

But parades are nothing like this. They're happy, not dangerous.

The boy leads their row, taller, his strides bigger and stronger. I watch as he pulls on the girls on either side of him. And how one of the girls pulls on Angelika's linked arm. I see Angelika straining to maintain her stride. To me, it's obvious her gait isn't like the others and that Angelika's hip is bothering her.

But most of all, it's her simple presence that threatens to choke me. People are being arrested. Only months ago, an entire group of students was executed for their anti-Nazi posters. People disappear every day, never to be seen again.

"Eyes and ears," as Papa says.

It doesn't take much to hear or see Angelika today.

Inside the fountain, I step in front of Marianne to block her view of my sister. If only there was a way to step in front of all the storm troopers or all the other Nazi officials here or any other Nazi supporters within the crowd.

I look again, my eye catching on the brown-haired girl next to Angelika. Beneath their hats and scarves, who they are isn't instantly obvious. I'm thankful for that. I don't know who the girl is, but my sister's new hair matches hers, sticking out from beneath their identical hats.

My guess is the girl is Sophie.

My guess is that Angelika recently cut her hair to look like Sophie's.

My sister's new hairstyle isn't the issue, though.

Anger spikes in me because this girl protected my sister at the factory, only to yank her down the street in a protest.

I close my eyes, breathing in the cold air, my mind numb to what I should do to save my sister. But then everyone in the street scatters. I frantically search for Angelika, but I lose her in the commotion. More than one body is facedown against the ground, the knees of storm troopers on their backs. The other protesters leap over them, flee around them, shouting out final protests.

The square is thinning of people, leaving Marianne and me huddled together in the drained fountain. Suddenly I feel exposed. Then the angriest voice I've ever heard screams at us, "Get out of here!"

Marianne and I run the entire way home, shutting my apartment door behind us within minutes. We're still breathing heavily, my lungs on fire from the cold air, when Papa comes in. His eyes are huge. Within two big steps, he has his hands behind my head and Marianne's and pulls us toward his chest.

"Angelika?" he asks.

I shake my head. "I haven't seen her."

But I have. Lying is easier when I can't see his face. But he'd be disappointed in her. If not disappointed, then certainly worried sick.

I'm definitely disappointed.

I'm also worried sick.

Papa releases us from our hugs, glancing back at our closed apartment door. He says softly, "She'll be home soon," and then he strides toward his radio.

It's static. Every signal he tries is static.

Tigerlily enters the room, stretching between each step. She lets out a single meow.

Papa lifts the phone but frowns.

"What is it?" I ask.

"Telephone isn't working either." He shakes his head. "Heh. The governor apparently doesn't want anyone hearing or talking about what happened today."

I glance at the door. "What will happen to those who were arrested?" I ask.

Papa's eyes drift to the door, too. "It's not for you girls to worry about."

Marianne says, "They should be punished for ruining the event. We lost all our donations, too."

The door flinging open saves Papa and me from having to respond.

Angelika is out of breath. Her cheeks have a rosy glow. She's doing her best to hide a smile, but she's failing.

She sees us all standing there. A few moments of awkward silence pass, then: "Well, I'll get supper started."

That's all she says.

I have a lot I want to say to her.

But I can't, not in front of Marianne. Maybe not even in front of Papa.

We talk about the stupidest stuff while we eat.

Marianne wants new uniforms. Papa talks about his curriculum. Angelika mentions some theory she learned in her philosophy class.

Papa says how Angelika's friend Sophie seems bright.

I pause from chewing to twist my mouth at the mention of *her*. There was a time I thought Angelika was the bright one, but now I'm not so sure. Why would she join Sophie in a dangerous protest? Talking about Hitler at home, in private, is one thing. But Papa said we have to keep acting like normal, out in the world. It's too dangerous otherwise.

What we don't talk about is today's assembly turned illegal protest, which feels like the biggest elephant in the room. We also don't talk about the war or if we think there will be a fifth White Rose leaflet or if England will fill our skies with their bombers again.

Despite us not talking about anything serious, I want to know: "Marianne, how's your mama finding her search for a new apartment?"

Angelika jokes, "Trying to get rid of your best friend?"

I glare at my sister. "Of course not." But I hope no one notices how it takes me another breath to look my best friend in the eye.

"Good, I think," Marianne says. "I feel like she's looked at so many apartments. The problem is the entire neighborhood is doing the same thing. Then there are other evacuees coming here."

That's right. We had two new girls at our last JM

meeting. I couldn't imagine first losing my home, then relocating to a new city, only to find myself in the middle of a riot.

Papa says, "Well, your welcome here won't wear out."

Unless the bombers come back and set their sights here. Then we'd be added to the list of home hunters.

My stomach's in knots by the time we push back our chairs and get ready for bed. Papa's not even sure if there will be school tomorrow.

In bed, I worry about the unknowns, my sister's safety high on that list. I wait until I hear Marianne breathing soundly. Then I creep into my sister's room and over to her bed.

"Angelika," I whisper. It's not the friendliest whisper. I add a shake of her arm.

"What do you want, Brigitte?" she mumbles, waking up.

I exhale, trying to temper my annoyance. "I want to know why you felt the need to march like that today."

The glow from a streetlight seeps in through her blinds. She keeps her eyes closed, but she licks her lips. "You saw me?"

"*Anyone* could have seen you. I hope it was only me who recognized you. There I was, collecting donations for a war and a man I don't believe in. Papa still buys their newspapers. You went to Ulm. We're playing parts here, Angelika. Is all of that for nothing, when you're out there protesting?"

That gets my sister to open her eyes. "Look, I'm sorry. I didn't plan to march. No one did. It just happened. You were there, obviously. You heard Herr Giesler. You saw how people responded. There were a lot of unhappy people. I happened to be one of them."

Everything she says sounds rehearsed and not very sorry. How many times has she run this confrontation through her head? Does she have various versions? One for me? One for Papa? One for the Gestapo?

"And what if you were arrested?" I hiss. "What if they found out you had polio? What then, Angelika?"

"Calm down." She laughs. Actually laughs. "You're acting like my mother."

I want to slap her. I want to scream that she's lucky she once had a mother to even speak of. "We only have a father," I spit, keeping my voice low, controlled. "If you bring suspicion onto our family, Papa could get taken away. It could get you taken away. Is that what you want?"

"Of course not."

Tears moisten my eyes, replacing my anger. "We're all we have."

"I know." She frees her hand from beneath her blanket to take mine. Her voice softens. "You're right. I'm sorry. I got caught up in the moment. It's just that Sophie is so brave. She stands up for what she believes in. Today, I felt brave, too."

"Angelika—"

"I know, the safety of our family . . ."

"Yes," I plead. "Promise me you won't do something like that again. Promise me, Angelika."

She squeezes my hand. "I promise. I'll be smarter."

I carry her promise with me back to my bed, holding it close in the darkness.

CHAPTER 16

I knew it was only a matter of time. A few days have passed since the assembly, my stomach remaining in knots, and then—boom—a bombing. It's not a massive air raid, and it's not exactly close to us, but the bombs were dropped last night over our country's capital of Berlin.

Papa's by his radio. Both the telephone and radio are working again. He has the volume lower than usual on account of our houseguest. Even with it being months since the last air raid, it feels so familiar to see him there, hunched forward like that, staring at the brown box as if he can visualize each word leaving the speakers.

The past months haven't exactly been filled with

comfort. The dangers of more bombings, of more leaflets, of more opportunities for my family to slip up, were a constant needling in my head. But I'd take that uncertainty any day over days where bombs fall again from the sky.

When we all leave the house for our different schools, Papa says to us, "Be mindful."

"I can walk with you," I offer Marianne. She'll be by herself, whereas Papa, Angelika, and I go in the same direction.

"No," she says. "I'll be fine."

At lunchtime, we both happen to arrive home at the same time. She's at the other end of our block, headed toward me. I wave. She waves. And I smile that she seems okay. Before going inside, she nods to the mailbox. "Think the mail's come?"

I shrug. "Maybe. Papa will get it later."

Marianne bites her lip. "Couldn't we get it now?"

"My papa always gets it."

Marianne says, "Well, you've got two working hands."

I do, but I'm nervous about using them to open that

mailbox. The bombings took a break, only to begin again. What if the leaflets did, too? What if there's one in my mailbox right now? I can imagine Marianne's mouth falling open and then questions spilling out:

Have you gotten all the leaflets?

Have you been lying to me?

Does your papa believe these blasphemous words?

Does Angelika?

Do you?

How could you?

Do you want your family torn apart?

Do you want your papa to be taken away, never to be seen again?

"Brigitte," Marianne says firmly. "Please get the mail. My mama gave Papa your address so he can write me directly. If there's something in there from him, I want it right now, not when your papa gets home."

When my papa gets home. Because in mere hours, he will walk through our door. He's not fighting on the Russian front. But her papa is. "All right," I say.

I hold my breath. I open the box. There's nothing inside. The mail hasn't come yet.

Marianne sighs. "Guess your papa will get the mail once it comes."

"Yes." It's all I say.

After our JM meeting, Marianne and I walk in to the smell of ground pork and spices. Papa is laying down the mail on the table.

"Anything for me?" Marianne asks.

"Sorry, my chamomile. Let's hope for tomorrow, yes?"

I grin inwardly at the nickname he's given her. "Chamomiles are lovely flowers," he told me a few weeks ago. "But boy do they spread easily. Much like Marianne's possessions around our apartment."

I think it's ironic he gave her the nickname that I once used when I thought of us JM girls being Hitler's flowers—with their white petals and yellow heads. Even though Marianne's hair is brown, she's very much Hitler's flower.

But my papa's a good man and kind to my best friend. I offer him a smile now, but I stop short. Marianne's mail may not have come, but I see him nod toward his alcove. *We* got mail. That fifth leaflet . . . it's here.

The White Rose has begun their efforts again. For a while now, I've wondered who is behind the leaflets, if I've passed that person on the streets, if we've stood beside each other in the market, if they've sat in Papa's seats at the university. And what of their name? *White Rose.*

Depending on who is asked, roses stand for different things.

Some say innocence and purity.

Others say it's a symbol of new beginnings, or of a goodbye.

Papa mentioned one time when he was Mama Hiccuping how she wore a rose in her hair during their wedding. He tapped my nose as he said, "A single white rose—just one—means love."

We are beyond a single White Rose leaflet. They have sent five. I wish they were done. I can all but feel the leaflet in Papa's alcove. White roses may be a symbol of innocence, yet that flyer, with its anti-Hitler words, is so dangerous to be sitting there. And even more dangerous for us to hold in our hands, as if covered in hidden thorns. What will this one say?

That night, I can hardly wait for Marianne to fall asleep. I'm nervous, yet intrigued, but also hesitant to read the words. The pads of Tigerlily's paws are soundless. I try to mimic her with my feet. My hands are a different story. I flutter them, whirling them around from excitement because I'm about to be included in one of the midnight meetings Papa and Angelika used to have while I slept. Or while they thought I slept.

I find my father and sister in Papa's alcove.

Papa's greeting is silent. He opens his arm for me and I sidle in next to him. The first four leaflets were titled LEAFLETS OF THE WHITE ROSE but this one is slightly different. It says LEAFLETS OF THE RESISTANCE.

I whisper, "Is it still from the White Rose?"

Angelika nods.

"What's it say?"

Papa points to a line.

HITLER CANNOT WIN THE WAR; HE CAN ONLY PROLONG IT.

I ask, "And you agree?"

Papa rubs his forehead. "There was a time I thought he'd win. But things are bad in Russia. Some of our army is trapped there. What's worse, Hitler's generals have abandoned them. They're not trying to get them home to Germany."

Angelika shakes her head. "Look," she says. I don't want to. My head's still stuck on the fact our brothers and uncles and papas are being trapped there. Maybe papas like Marianne's. But Angelika is tapping her finger. "The White Rose says the war's already been lost. Not that one battle in Russia, but the entire war. An invasion of Germany is coming. Britain, the United States, Russia, and France. They've all allied against Germany. That's a lot of countries against our country, especially with the Americans' astounding numbers. Our armies are retreating. That's what it says here. And read this. It's word for word what Hitler has said . . ."

I WILL FIGHT TO THE LAST MAN.

It's chilling. Those words. I recall other words, too—from a newspaper headline I saw weeks ago:

HATE IS OUR PRAYER—AND VICTORY OUR REWARD.

But hate hasn't gotten our country anywhere, except in the middle of a war the White Rose insists we will lose to the Allies. That is not victory.

I recognize this. Why can't the grown-ups or the leader of our country?

I lean into Papa. He's a grown-up who understands. "What about Marianne's papa?" I ask. "He's in Russia."

"I know, my cornflower. We can only hope and pray he's safe."

Safe. Is anyone safe? I sigh, though it's more of a shudder. "So what are we supposed to do?"

"Well," Papa begins, and rubs his eyes. "The White Rose suggests we disassociate ourselves with Hitler while the war is still going on."

I ask, "Disassociate?"

"Detach. Separate. Our country will be badly judged when this is all over. We should distance ourselves from Hitler and his beliefs."

"But how can we do that?"

Papa's eyes are sad. "I'm not certain. Not yet. But you two flowers leave that to me. Okay?"

"Okay," I whisper.

Angelika nods, but her attention is still on the leaflet.

At the bottom it says, SUPPORT THE RESISTANCE. DISTRIBUTE THE LEAFLETS!

I can all but see that exclamation mark reflecting in her eyes.

"Angelika," I begin. I'm ready to remind her of her promise. I'll tell Papa about the assembly and how she was one of the protestors if I have to.

I turn at a sound.

Tigerlily rounds the corner. Whew. She's probably looking for me, unable to sleep directly on the bed. She needs me between herself and the comfy mattress.

"Let's get some sleep," Papa says.

I'll try.

He begins pushing us down the hall. But I notice how Angelika discreetly reaches back and takes the leaflet. I narrow my eyes at her, but I don't say anything. Papa will track it down. He'll burn this one, just like the others.

I get into bed. I must fall sleep at some point, because when I next open my eyes, Marianne is standing over me.

Her arms are crossed.

Her lips are pursed.

She's mad.

She says, "I saw your little family meeting last night."

Chapter 17

My first thought is *no*.

No, no, no, no, no.

We were so careful to keep everything hush-hush while Marianne's been staying with us. The radio. Angelika's disability. Any anti-Hitler talk. Any real talk of the war.

All our efforts have been for nothing.

Marianne shakes her head. "Your family gets those leaflets." She says it with such conviction and disgust: Your family—*pause*—gets—*pause*—those leaflets.

It's not posed as a question that I can deny.

She saw us. She heard us.

I stare at her, not knowing what to say. I wish I could disappear beneath my covers, then my bed would sink through the floor and into the cellar. From there, I could escape. Marianne wouldn't be looking at me like this anymore.

I know I need to speak next. She's waiting, her arms still crossed. Now she juts out her hip. Her foot is tapping. My goodness, her nostrils even flare.

Where is Tigerlily? She left me here all alone. I bet even the cat sees how angry Marianne is. I bet the cat hid somewhere.

I lick my lips, swallow, and sit up in bed. "The leaflets have been mailed here, yes. But they've been mailed so many places across München."

She says, "Not to my family. My papa's in Russia. He fights *with* the Führer. And he's fine. Just fine. The Führer is going to win. I don't care what those White Rose people say."

I breathe, in and out. I'm at a loss for how to respond to Marianne's certainty.

I feel foolish that I'm still in bed. I kick my feet out of my sheets and stand.

Marianne takes a step away from me. "You told me your family didn't get the leaflets. You lied to me."

"I was afraid," I say honestly. "Everyone looks at Rita like she's a criminal."

"It's forbidden to have them!"

"We only received it," I say in a soft voice. Then I think how Angelika took the leaflet with her last night. I look in the direction of her room. Where is she now? Where is Papa? What time is it, even? It's still dark outside.

"No." Marianne's eyes are wild. "You were reading the leaflet. I caught the three of you talking about those lies. In the middle of the night. That's more than receiving it."

I want to say something. But what? She's not wrong. We were reading it and she clearly heard us talking about how the White Rose thinks her papa is going to lose. Of course she sees their words as lies. Elisabeth screamed in our meeting how the White Rose were liars. And of course Marianne sees me talking about it as a betrayal. I feel for her. I feel for Marianne so much, but I have to think of my family, too, so I say what I want to say most. I'm desperate. "Please don't tell anyone."

She's silent.

The silence is awkward and I drop my gaze. It lands on her bag. It's bulging, fully packed, everything barely fitting since she's acquired more while living with us. "What are you doing? Are you leaving?"

"Yes." To punctuate her point, she turns and picks up her bag. "I already called my mama."

"You did?" There's fear in my voice. "You didn't tell her why you're leaving, did you? Marianne. You didn't say anything over the phone, right?"

Her face scrunches. "Calm down. What's your problem?"

My problem is that *things* can be heard over the phone line. I take a calming breath. "I only want to know what you told your mama."

"Just that I want to go home," she says through her teeth. But then as if she realizes she doesn't have a home anymore, she corrects herself. "I don't want to be here."

"Okay," I say slowly. It's like the fuse has been lit on Marianne and she's about to explode. Where's Papa? I wish he were here to help defuse this situation. "Let's go," I offer. "I'll walk with you."

"No," she says. "I'm going by myself."

With that, her braid whips like a weapon as she turns and stomps out of my room. She stomps down the hall. She stomps out the front door, only pausing long enough to rip her coat from our tree-shaped coat rack.

Quietly, I wrap my own big coat around myself.

I follow her outside. The streets are dark and quiet. Being outside this early, before curfew has been lifted, feels dangerous. But I can't let her go across town all alone. She must know I'm behind her, but she doesn't speak to me or acknowledge me. Her arms only pump as she speed walks.

My shoulders relax a fraction when sunlight starts to illuminate the shadows. Other people emerge, as the morning comes alive. The first streetcar passes. Marianne boards the next one but keeps her face turned away when I take a seat in the row behind her.

At her uncle's stop, the sun is beginning to fully peek

over the buildings. I don't see anyone else on her street, but I smell the aroma of freshly baked bread.

"Marianne," I finally say before she climbs the steps to her uncle's building. "I'm sorry."

She spins around. "Why?" she asks, her tone harsh. "Sorry you got caught? Sorry about whatever else you're hiding from me?"

I press my lips together. "I can't stop you from telling your mama about what my family receives. But I hope you won't. I hope you'll think about the consequences." I only add one more word. "Adelita."

She stares at me. She doesn't say a word. Marianne only stares. Then she disappears into the building's lobby.

I pull my coat around me tighter. I stand there for another minute, imagining what she's saying to her mama. The problem is, I can't imagine. I don't know what she'll say. I've changed. Our relationship has changed.

I rush home, grateful the sun is up now and curfew has been lifted, grateful that my coat covers my nightgown so I don't get any curious glances.

When I burst in the door, Papa's and Angelika's voices come from the kitchen. I hurry there.

Papa says, "There you are, my cornflower. I was so worried."

"Burn it. Right now," I command my sister. "I saw you take the leaflet last night. Burn it. Marianne overheard us in the alcove. She knows we get the leaflets."

Chapter 18

Angelika burns the pamphlet.

I watch, the entire time, until the White Rose's pamphlet is nothing but ashes. I don't enjoy burning their words. But it's necessary.

Angelika doesn't watch. She retreats to her bedroom, leaving behind a chilliness despite the fire.

Papa slips out, too, not saying a word. I don't realize he's left the apartment until he returns. Oddly, he rushes to his alcove, discreetly emptying his pockets into one of the drawers. Then he goes straight to the radio.

I tear my eyes from the drawers, wondering what Papa is up to. At the radio, he holds his head between his hands, listening. I close my eyes, as if that'll make all that's going on disappear—Marianne, whatever

Papa just hid, the White Rose—and I ask, "More bombings?"

Yes. The broadcast talks of two more cities. Both are coastal cities that have suffered previous air raids.

Once Papa stands again, I ask, "What did you put in the alcove?"

"Money. It'll be good to have close by if we need it quickly . . ."

Papa trails off, but I know what he's not saying.

In case we need the money to quickly leave München.

What a sinking feeling. So is the idea of going to my next JM meeting, but I go like a good Nazi would. I could tick off on my fingers how we are good Nazis. With the exception of how we don't actually want to be Nazis.

At the clubhouse, I drag my feet to my regular seat, but Marianne won't even look at me when I sit next to her. The order of our chairs used to always be the same: Adelita, Rita, me, and Marianne. A breath later, Marianne leaves her seat and takes Adelita's old chair.

If my stomach wasn't already jostled, that certainly does the trick. Marianne takes Adelita's empty chair as if it's nothing, as if it's not vacant because of *her.*

The other girls notice the seat hopping, and while their eyes go wide, no one says a word, including Rita, who is now sandwiched between Marianne and me. Not that I'm expecting Rita to talk to me. Her cold shoulder hasn't thawed, whether it be at school or here.

Elisabeth enters the circle, taking her normal position at the center. She has something to say to us. Or rather, she asks us, "I've learned there's been a new leaflet from that resistance group." Elisabeth won't even say their name. "Has anyone's family received it?"

My stomach drops into my brown shoes.

I pray Marianne's voice doesn't break the room's silence. But I'll deny anything she says about me or my family. That's what Papa told me to do. Deny, deny, deny. Then come straight home. Elisabeth and Frau Weber know Rita's family has gotten the leaflets, Papa reminded me, yet none of them have been arrested. But could it be because it was sent to her family's barroom? Whereas the leaflets we receive come to our home? Does that make a difference?

"Rita?" Elisabeth asks.

Rita's knuckles turn white.

"No," she says, yet her voice shakes. Whether it's because everyone is staring at her or because she is heeding my advice to lie, I'm not sure. "My family didn't receive that leaflet."

Elisabeth locks eyes with her.

Rita swallows.

"You're certain?" Elisabeth asks.

"Yes."

Silence fills the room again for what feels like forever. Then finally: "What wonderful news," Elisabeth says, including all the girls in this declaration by slowly turning her body. "Rita's family is no longer being targeted."

A few smiles break out on faces. One girl gives a quiet clap. Another girl is utterly relieved for Rita, releasing a slow breath.

I'm happy for Rita, too, but now my worry shifts again to myself. I'm terrified of what Marianne might do. Or rather, what she might say. I risk a glance at her, but with Rita between us, I only see the redness of Rita's cheeks.

I tuck my hands between my knees, hoping Elisabeth

will abandon her leaflet questioning and carry on with our meeting. That's when I see Marianne's hand pop up over Rita's head.

No, no, no.

My next thought: *There's not a single leaflet in our apartment. There's no proof.*

"Yes, Marianne?"

In my head, I'm already practicing an expression of surprise. I'll raise my eyebrows. My mouth will form an O shape. Then, I'll let out a laugh, as if what Marianne says is so unbelievable it's comical. I'll have to really sell it. Elisabeth loves Marianne.

"It's just that," Marianne begins in a slower-than-usual cadence, "I'm curious about the leaflet, if that's okay to ask."

It's the last thing I expect to hear.

Elisabeth's shocked face resembles what I'd practiced in my own head. Except she doesn't laugh. Her head cocks. "You're curious?"

Marianne's voice cracks. "Only about what it says this time. We discussed the *lies* in the others."

"Yes, the lies," Elisabeth emphasizes. "I haven't read the filthy words. But trust me that whatever is on that paper is traitorous and flat-out erroneous."

Every head in our circle nods, including my own. Not to what Elisabeth said. Never anymore to what Elisabeth says. My head bobs to reassure myself that Rita didn't spill the beans about me warning her to keep quiet. And that Marianne didn't reveal my family's secrets, when she could have.

But she still can. I still worry.

The coming days bring plenty more to worry about. One day as Papa listens to his radio in the other room, I hear the strong, loud voice coming from the speakers falter. The transmission gets garbled. I run to listen with him. The roaring sound of planes and distant boom of bombs comes clearly even through the radio. I cover my mouth and Papa pulls me in against him.

"What was that?" I ask.

Papa responds quietly, resigned to telling me because I already heard. "Hitler's right-hand man was speaking to an audience in Berlin. They were bombed *while* he was speaking." The radio changes to static and the white noise seeps into my bones as I stare at the machine.

"Berlin was bombed again?" This is the second time this month. "During a speech? But it's daytime." I look up at Papa, hoping for an explanation. So far, bombings have only happened under the cover of night. Papa is as shocked as I am. I imagine planes marring our blue sky in broad daylight. I imagine the bombs falling like deadly candies over the large crowd listening to the speech like good Nazis.

My arms are covered in goose bumps, and I have an urge to flee to the cellar even though Berlin is hundreds and hundreds and hundreds of kilometers away.

"We're safe," Papa says. "The siren would be going off if we weren't."

I search his face for a lie.

But Papa's gotten good at hiding what he really thinks.

A few days later, we're at the radio again and I'm watching Papa's face again. We're not listening to Germany's broadcast, but England's. It's illegal. Very illegal. I'm glad Marianne's not here, especially with what the broadcasters are saying. The Battle of Stalingrad is over. Germany has surrendered.

We've lost in Russia.

What does that mean for Marianne's papa? Will he come home now? Or is he one of the men who were abandoned and trapped there weeks ago? I cringe to even think it, but he could be a prisoner of war. He could still be in Russia. And I wonder, "Was Hitler captured?"

Papa laughs. It's not a funny ha-ha laugh, but one that's more sarcastic. "Hitler isn't anywhere near Russia. He doesn't fight. His air raid shelter has a theater, for goodness' sake."

How nice for him. Fury builds within me. Hitler proclaimed he'd fight until the last man. And he nearly did. Except Hitler stopped fighting. He abandoned his men. From the safety of his hidey-hole, Hitler threw up his hands and he chose to leave his remaining men to die in Russia.

The White Rose has been right all along.

I swallow, but the lump in my throat feels larger than Russia.

And now I dread seeing my best friend even more. Fortunately, I don't have a JM event for another two days.

The morning of, I drag my feet on the way to school. Papa and Angelika are ahead of me. I kick pebbles as I go, my head down—and walk straight into Papa's backside.

Papa and Angelika have stopped. Everyone has. There's a sea of people, all gawking at something on a brick wall. What that is, I have to elbow myself between Papa and Angelika to find out.

Then my mouth drops open.

"Down with Hitler," I read aloud. Papa shushes me. I slap a hand over my mouth. He shakes his head, as if he's disgusted by the big, bold letters in black tar. Even though he's not.

I lean forward, looking down the avenue. Those three words are repeated again and again and again. My God, it looks like it's repeated a hundred times, all the way down the wall.

I overhear a whisper: "The Kittelbach Pirates, you think?"

It makes sense, at first blush. Everyone knows about

the Kittelbach Pirates. As the stories go, the kids are between my age and Angelika's. They hang out, listen to jazz and dance the swing. The girls wear lipstick and paint their nails. They do everything Hitler is against us young people doing. But then they also do stuff like beat up Nazi officials and write graffiti on walls.

Graffiti just like this.

The thing is, the Kittelbach Pirates are up north, not anywhere near us in southern Germany. But the White Rose is here in München. Are they responsible instead?

I look up at Papa, then my sister, prepared to whisper my question, when I see my sister mouthing something to someone.

It's Sophie, the girl from the protest, even wearing the same hat and scarf.

Sophie subtly shakes her head. She mouths something back to my sister.

I've always been horrendous at lip reading. I remember one time during a JM meeting, I frustrated the bejesus out of Marianne when she was trying to tell me something and . . . none of that is important right now.

Angelika mouths something back, but ever so quietly, she says it, too. Just loud enough for my eyes and ears to make out, "Hans?"

Didn't Angelika mention Sophie's brother was named Hans? Is *he* responsible for this display of anti-Nazism?

Sophie shrugs, but she also raises her brows. Is that a yes or no? I don't know.

Angelika smiles. Sophie's mouth turns up ever so slightly in response, that subtle grin remaining on her face as her eyes turn to the graffiti.

Papa tugs on my arm. "Let's keep going. The Gestapo will be here any minute to ask questions."

Papa jostles my sister and me forward. Others are walking on, too. Some still stand there, whispering, pointing, covering their mouths in surprise, and shaking their heads in anger.

I wonder if all those who shake their head are really mad. Or do they do it like Papa did—for show?

Another crowd has gathered outside the university.

There's more graffiti, this time written over the building's entrance.

But this time it says FREEDOM!

Even if Papa agrees, he's flustered. His fingers grip into my shoulder. His other hand is on Angelika's. "We'll walk you to school today," he tells me. Papa guides us away. With the recent protest, the ongoing leaflets, and now this graffiti, I'm shocked Papa doesn't guide us right out of München.

Chapter 19

In truth, Papa wants to. He wants us to leave.

"I wrote a letter to Uncle Otto," Papa tells my sister and me after school. He asked me to come home right after my last class. I skipped today's JM meeting.

"Uncle Otto?" I ask.

"Yes. I think it's time for us to leave."

I glance at the alcove, where he's been squirreling away money.

"It's time for us to leave Germany?" Angelika asks. "You want us to go to Uncle Otto's in Switzerland?"

Papa nods.

I'm in shock. I guessed Papa wanted us out of München, but I assumed we'd go somewhere safer within Germany. Where . . . I wasn't sure. I was waiting for Papa to tell us where. But even the idea of leaving München and this apartment and my friends and my life here gives me enough of a heavy heart. I never expected him to say Switzerland.

I have to sit down. But as soon as I do, I realize I've picked the "bad news" chair. I stand as quick as I can, as if that'll make a difference. "Why Switzerland?" I ask. "Why not somewhere else in Germany?" I've never left Germany before. Angelika did, when she stayed with Uncle Otto to recover from her polio. But I'm not sure Papa has ever left either.

"Switzerland is a neutral country. They never get involved or take sides in wars. It's where many refugees go."

I ask, "Refugees?" while thinking I understand: an evacuee.

"It's someone who leaves their country to escape something."

"Like when I was sick," Angelika says, her arms crossed and all her weight to her good side.

"And now to escape Hitler," I say, sadness in my voice.

"Yes, but we're not going anywhere yet," Papa says.

"Soon. After arrangements are made. Ever since that last leaflet, I've been thinking about where we could go to disassociate from Hitler and keep our family safe. Hopefully Uncle Otto understands my letter. I told him I was giving our RSVP to his wedding."

"But he's not getting married," I say.

"No."

Oh. Papa's scared someone will read the mail.

"You don't think they'd let us leave otherwise?" I ask.

He nods. "It'd be a very quick way to brand us as traitors."

And not supportive of Hitler.

"This goes without saying," Papa begins, "but I'll say it anyway. No one can know our plans. Understood?"

I've never understood so much before in my life.

I'm running late. I'm home for lunch when I realize I never packed a neckerchief for my JM meeting after school. I'd skip it if a) I hadn't already skipped one recently—I don't want people to start noticing and become suspicious of where my loyalties lie—and b) it meant I could simply come home after school. But now that Papa is in full-blown Papa Bear mode, he wants me to come to his boring office after school on the days I don't have a JM event, which has been the past two days.

So I'll go to my meeting. So I'll see Marianne. She still hasn't spoken to me. As far as I know, she still hasn't spoken *about* me either.

But first, my neckerchief. I search my room. I look inside my shirts, in case it got stuck there in the wash. In the past, I've found socks and underwear that way, but I have no such luck today for my neckerchief. I move on to Angelika's drawers—and victory—that's where I find my neckerchief, stuck between two of her folded shirts. I grab it and push her drawer closed. In a heartbeat, I leap to catch one of the potted plants teetering on the edge of her dresser.

I already imagine the mess of dirt and petals on the floor. Instead, the pot lands in my hands. I'm shaking my head at my clumsiness when I notice something strange, something peeking out from the disrupted soil.

I push aside more of the dirt. Eyes scrunched in confusion, I pull free a strip of stamps. When I unfold it, it becomes a sheet of rows and rows of stamps. Fifty of them.

My goose bumps are back.

Why does my sister need fifty stamps?

Better question: Why does my sister need to *hide* fifty stamps?

Chapter 20

I return to school after my lunch break, neckerchief found, but for the remainder of my classes, all I can think about are those hidden stamps.

Angelika isn't much for sending letters.

No one in our family is.

Letters are necessities, like when Angelika was in Ulm or how Papa reached out to Uncle Otto.

But fifty stamps?

I weave in and out of people on the sidewalk, toward the JM clubhouse.

It'd take Angelika fifty years to use all those stamps. Unless she wasn't the one using them. Unless she bought them for someone else. Unless she was hiding them until those somebodies were ready to use them. The *someone* and *somebodies* don't take much brainpower to figure out, but I won't allow myself to fully think it.

Because fully thinking that my sister is in cahoots with the . . .

Angelika promised she wouldn't get involved in more protests.

She promised she'd be more careful.

For my sister, did *careful* simply mean being better at hiding what she was doing?

In my anger I brush by a gentleman on the sidewalk, then mumble my apologies.

It's not as if Angelika has been discreet about Sophie. Every night at supper it's *Sophie this* and *Sophie that.*

Sophie is Angelika's new Johanna. And while I'm happy my sister has a best friend to laugh with again, I wish it was a girl whose papa wasn't in jail, who didn't openly protest along the boulevard, who didn't smile at graffiti denouncing Hitler, who isn't part of the White Rose.

There, I thought it.

Sophie has her hand in those leaflets. I just have a feeling.

So does her brother Hans. And I also realize something about the timing of those leaflets. They stopped when Hans left for Russia, then resumed again when he and Sophie were back at the university. Sophie and Hans are the White Rose, or they're at least part of it.

But the question is . . . is my sister involved, beyond buying stamps?

Even that is dangerous. "Take her away" or "put her in prison" dangerous.

None of it makes me feel good. My feet hit harder than usual on the sidewalk as I swing open the door of my JM clubhouse.

I'm not in the mood to be here. I'm not in the mood to be home either. I'd probably look daggers at my sister. I'm certainly not in the mood for Marianne's and Rita's never-ending cold shoulders.

It's why I'm so shocked when Marianne approaches me.

"Hi," she says. Then her head tilts. "Are you okay?"

"I'm fine."

Saying it makes me feel even worse. Because I'm not fine. And I should be able to tell my best friend that my papa wants us to leave Germany or that I found stamps in my sister's room—and *know* that she won't tell a soul.

What I really want to do is ask if she's told a soul about us receiving the leaflets . . . that Angelika may have a hand in. I can't help it; my teeth grind.

"You don't look fine," Marianne says.

I answer with, "How are you?"

"Good. Russia is over so my papa should be coming home soon. In fact, it's why I wanted to talk to you. I can't find my necklace he gave me. You know, the one with the horseshoe."

I hope so—about her papa coming home. But then that's why she's talking to me: because she needs something. I know the pendant. "I'll look for it tonight—"

Elisabeth enters the room and Marianne reacts. I once watched a toad jump down by the river. The toad began still, completely motionless. I wasn't sure it was ever going to move. I blinked. Then—bang—it was gone. It jumped so suddenly and went so far that my eyes lost track of it. It was dizzying.

That's Marianne.

She left like a toad.

Somehow she's well across the room. And when it comes time to take our seats, she chooses Adelita's old chair once again. I'm next to Rita, not as if she'll talk to me.

But then she does.

"Thank you," she says.

"Thank me?" I say in surprise.

She whispers, "For your advice. For months I felt like"—she nods toward the others in our circle of chairs—"have been watching me. Questioning me. But they don't anymore now that . . ."

That she lied about her family receiving the last White Rose leaflet.

I smile at her. "Good."

She grins back.

Who's not smiling at me is the enormous portrait of Hitler on the wood-paneled wall. I get the chills.

"Is everything okay?" Rita whispers.

That's a loaded question. "Yeah."

"I mean," she says, and she mouths the next part, "with Marianne."

Tears prick my eyes. "I don't know."

Elisabeth claps for everyone to quiet down, and every girl reacts by sitting properly. Knees together. Backs straight. Hands in our laps. Elisabeth's gaze lingers on me a moment longer than usual and my armpits grow sweaty.

At the end of the meeting, I say my goodbyes to Rita and the other girls, minus Marianne. It's apparently only okay to talk to me when she wants something.

On my way home, pettiness fills me, and I tell myself I'm not going to look for her horseshoe. But I know I will, and when I get home, I ask Papa, "Have you seen Marianne's necklace? The pendant is a horseshoe."

"No. She spoke to you?"

I nod.

"Do you think she's spoken to others?"

He means about me. I shrug. I'm not certain. But I remember Elisabeth's prolonged look. And Marianne has made it clear, with her toad-like disappearance and her permanent new chair, she doesn't want to be associated with me.

"Okay," Papa says, the little crease between his eyebrows lingering.

I begin my search for the stupid necklace. I twist my lips and look between the couch cushions. I check the bathroom, under my bed, behind my dresser. Tigerlily is on my heels the entire time. I stop. She stops, and then weaves between my legs.

The only place left to look is my sister's room.

It makes my heart beat faster. It shouldn't. Those stamps can't hurt me. They won't suddenly grow arms, legs, and teeth and attack me. They still make me nervous, though.

"We can do this, Tigerlily," I whisper, and scoop her up.

I go in. I start with Angelika's bed, placing Tigerlily there. She deems it her new nap spot. The horseshoe isn't there. It's not anywhere I look. But of course, I haven't gone near the dresser. I approach slowly, shaking my head at myself for acting so silly.

Just check the drawers and leave, I tell myself.

I begin checking, but my eyes drift up to the pot. As

much as I don't want to see the stamps, it's impossible not to lean onto my tiptoes and peek inside.

Yet I don't see the paper sticking out like I did before.

The soil has fingerprints in it, as if pressed down.

I look at Tigerlily. She's mid-yawn. I imagine she's telling me, "Angelika did it."

I rub my lips together, deliberating, questioning, then I give a testing poke with my finger. Feels normal to me. I poke again. I wiggle my finger. Turning the pot, I prod in other spots.

By the time I'm done, my calves are burning and the back of my neck prickles.

The stamps have vanished.

They were here merely hours ago. Now all fifty stamps are gone.

Did Angelika take them because of me? I put them back as best I could, but could she tell I found them? Or is it simply time to use them?

"Papa!" I yell, wiping my hand against my shirt as I leave my sister's room. I find him in the kitchen, stirring a pot.

"Find Marianne's necklace?"

“Papa,” I say, “where’s Angelika?”

“I told her I’d handle supper tonight. She rushed in earlier, then left again lickety-split.”

“Where’d she go?”

“Study group. Why, do you need her?”

No, I don’t need her. But I’m afraid somebody else might.

Chapter 21

It's nearly curfew and Angelika isn't home.

Before I know it, it's after Hitler's curfew and Angelika isn't home.

Why isn't Angelika home?

If the apartment weren't so quiet, I'd pace a path into my bedroom. But my footsteps would echo, so I sit on my bed and bounce my knee instead. I know one thing for sure: Angelika is *not* being careful. She is out there doing . . . I don't know what. Stamping leaflets? Writing them? Whatever she's doing can put her at risk. She could be arrested. Her secret—that the whole family has guarded for so long—could be discovered.

I drop my head into my hands—and squeeze.

The apartment's door clicks open and creaks closed.

My sister's trying to be quiet, but she's tired. I can tell by how her left footfall is louder than her right.

I stand to confront her. To say what, I don't know either. But then I hear Papa's bedroom door, his footsteps, then hushed words.

Their footsteps take them toward the kitchen.

I don't dare move, but I listen. I close my eyes, thinking that'll help me hear, but it doesn't. Their words are too quiet.

Until their footsteps come closer again, this time louder. Angelika's angry. Her voice also grows closer, clearer.

"So you're telling me I can't be her friend?"

"No," Papa whispers. "I never said that. I only said that she's older than you. She's an adult. Hans even more so."

"She's twenty-one. You act like she's ancient."

"You still have *teen* attached to your age. Sophie does not."

"Barely," Angelika hisses.

"It's there, my petunia."

"Don't." It's all my sister says, accented by the slam of her door. I stand halfway between my door and my bed, hearing the boom of her door echo in my mind.

In the morning, the three of us sit around the breakfast table, none of us uttering a word. I'm glad it's not me who has to tell Papa that something is going on with Angelika. He knows. And my earlier prediction that I'd shoot daggers at my sister comes true. Maybe I'm psychic.

I give her my worst.

But she's distracted.

I don't have school today—one of those days where teachers go but students don't—but Papa and Angelika do. Even after my insistence that I'm capable of staying home alone, Papa still shakes his head. "Get your coat and whatever else you'll need."

I groan but do as he says. I grab the deck of cards so I can play a solitaire game called German Patience. I have little doubt my patience will be tested sitting in Papa's office for hours.

"Hurry up!" Angelika yells.

"Hold your horses," I snap back, and pluck a book from a shelf.

There's more quietness on the way to the university. It's cold and I sink deeper into my coat. I tilt my head up when Angelika releases a low, amused snort. Along the boulevard, posters line the wall. For the past few days, those poor Russian women have been scrubbing and scrubbing to remove the black tar-like paint Hans and whoever else from the White Rose members used. Guess the Russian women were never able to fully remove the paint. Now, again and again, posters of Hitler's big old head plaster the wall to cover the propaganda against him.

I get the chills again.

It's as if Hitler is following me around the city.

At the university, the entrance has been freshly painted to hide the remaining graffiti. It now looks like the White Rose never touched it. Inside, they didn't. It's still the same marble stairs, the same archways, the same two huge statues of our old kings of Bavaria.

I wonder how the kings would feel now about the country they once ruled. I asked Papa about them before. The Wittelsbach dynasty ruled Bavaria for over seven hundred years, with the royal family living right here in München. Following a revolution, the final king ended their dynasty only twenty-five years ago. It ended right around the time the Romanovs of Russia were killed, ending their own three-hundred-year dynasty. Though rumors still exist about how not everyone in the Russian royal family died that day. Some believe the youngest princess, Anastasia, somehow survived. I like to think so.

Germany became a republic after the Wittelsbach dynasty fell. But Papa said the Wittelsbachs were anti-Nazi and they left Germany. Unfortunately they didn't get far enough. Some of their family members are now in concentration camps.

Students buzz around us as we enter the university.

There's an extra layer of tension in the air.

One girl is yanking on her hair, yammering to another girl about her physics exam—and the tension makes sense.

I forgot today is an exam day.

I wonder if that's another reason Papa was so upset with Angelika for returning home late.

The atrium is three stories high, with balconies on

the second and third levels that create a horseshoe shape. Students run toward their classrooms. Some take the steps two at a time. Beside Papa, I climb the steps, all the way to the top level. He leaves me at his office, then continues on to his lecture room.

I plop down into his chair and deal myself cards for solitaire. Chin on my fist, I begin to play. I'm lethargic, yawning as I flip and move the cards. But it's no wonder I'm exhausted with all that's going on with Hitler's eyes and ears, with Angelika's possible involvement in the White Rose, with Germany's loss in Russia, with the ongoing bombings, and with my uncertainty about Marianne's loyalty.

She's always been my right-hand woman, my confidante, my Freundin, my very best friend. I didn't ever think she'd be my fair-weather friend, but I don't see her sticking by me. She saw those leaflets and high-tailed it out of my apartment.

I sigh.

I complete my second game of solitaire and begin a third. Marianne always marvels at how I'm able to win. She always gets stuck with no more moves.

Noise breaks out in the halls.

Classes are switching.

I get up to move my legs and back, surprised at how much I need to stretch. My shoulders are tight. Too tight. I open Papa's door to see the hustle and bustle.

Outside the door there's a stack of papers.

I step closer and I release a puff of air.

LEAFLETS OF THE RESISTANCE

I see it plain as day at the top of the paper, the headline even bigger than usual.

I don't dare touch it. I'm not going to go near it.

But I walk to the balcony's edge to see how widely spread the stacks are. More and more people are emerging from classrooms.

People begin picking up the leaflets. Just as quickly, they drop them or pass them to someone else, reminding me of the party game called Hot Potato.

Across the atrium, on the other side of the third-floor balcony, I see Sophie. She's wearing her coat. A strange thing, if she's been here taking exams. She looks over her shoulder, ahead again, and then she pushes a stack of the leaflets that are perched on the thick railing.

My gaze drops for a split second—as the stack begins as one, then unfolds, separating—then I look back up to where Sophie pushed. She's gone.

The leaflets fall, scattering.

They look like little paper bombs, their words so dangerous, drifting and flittering down, down, down.

Upturned heads from the first floor await them.

Hands on the second floor reach out.

The leaflets begin to hit the ground. Some are caught. Those that find hands are instantly dropped, as if burning.

My knees quake at the sight of it all, that Angelika may somehow be part of this morning's display against Hitler. I search for her along the third-story balcony, then the second floor. Sophie is there. She *was* there; she disappears down the stairs toward the first floor. There's a boy with her. Hans, I bet. I also notice a small suitcase in her right hand.

Suddenly, there's a loud commotion. There's yelling. Screaming. I can't make it out. A student knocks into me and my belly presses hard against the balcony's banister. I respond by swinging back my elbow, the motion pushing me forward more. I look down, my eyes recognizing my sister.

I bite back her name, wanting to call it. She's holding one of the leaflets.

Drop it! I yell in my head.

Then I hear a loud boom of a voice scream, "Lock the doors!"

CHAPTER 22

The voice was commanding, echoing throughout the atrium's three floors.

All around me, people freeze. The only individuals making a mad dash toward the university's exit are the guards—and only to close the doors to lock everyone inside the building.

I push back from the railing, feeling as if I'm on display for anyone who looks up. I very well could backstep into Papa's office and lock that door. I do retreat, in fact. But I linger in Papa's doorway. If I go fully inside, I'll be safe, removed from whatever disorder Sophie and her brother have caused. Because there's no doubt in my mind that the stacks of leaflets were placed around the atrium by their hands, before Sophie released her little paper bombs on everyone below. I can't help but think of them that way.

And my sister is down on the first floor.

I don't trust her to drop the leaflet I saw her holding. I picture her getting caught with it, showing interest in it.

I don't trust her not to say something supportive of what the leaflet says. What that is, I don't know. I didn't read more than the title.

Or maybe Angelika will be more discreet, and she'll be overseen mouthing a conversation back and forth with Sophie. They are both down there.

I go down to the first floor, too.

There's no real commotion. Everyone stands in small groups, whispering. Guards of some sort stand shoulder to shoulder, blocking the building's exit.

While people look confused and maybe even unsure, given how their eyes dart around, it's Angelika roaming the room that makes her easy to find.

I grab her arm. Thank goodness there's no leaflet in her hand. "Angelika."

She stops. Sees me. "Have you seen my friend? Sophie. Short hair—"

"I know who she is."

"Good. Did you see her?"

I rub my lips together and scour the room for a moment.

"Brigitte."

"Yes, a few minutes ago, I saw her going toward the steps."

"Then where is she? Unless she got out before . . ."

"Angelika," I say softly. "Why did she carry a suitcase?"

"I can't say."

Okay, but what causes my hair to stand on end is how rehearsed Angelika's voice just sounded. Maybe she doesn't know, but I can't help feeling that I've heard that voice before. I bite my lip and watch Angelika watch the room. Finally, my sister smiles, a big old satisfied grin. "Come on," she says to me. "Let's go sit on the step while there are stairs left to sit on."

Papa finds us right after we sit down.

“Everyone okay?” he asks. But it’s all he asks or says. He’s satisfied with our nods. We’ll talk more around our supper table.

We’ve only been sitting for a minute or two when the two guards begin unlocking the university’s doors. I exhale. The atrium is cavernous. But I *feel* Angelika’s state of excitement about what I can only assume is a successful act of resistance. The White Rose pulled off spreading their words, this time in a very public way.

But I do wonder why Angelika had those stamps, unless more leaflets are going out in today’s mail and the university was just the first of two acts.

When the doors open, the closest students make to leave. They’re stopped.

Instead of anyone going out the doors, the Gestapo comes in.

Any type of comfort I found at the opening of those doors is slammed closed. It could’ve been normal officers, or even storm troopers, who walked in. It could’ve been more university guards. But no, it’s the Gestapo, Hitler’s secret police. Some of the Gestapo are even part of his inner circle. They do his dirty work.

Papa stiffens beside me. Angelika at least wipes the grin from her face. That grin made her look like the cat that caught the bird.

The Gestapo begins questioning people. There are a handful of them and hundreds of us. I don't know what they're asking, but I can guess.

When a Gestapo man gets to us, he does a double take, perhaps at seeing someone so young at the university. His eyes immediately narrow. Papa stands to meet him. Papa's hand is on Angelika's shoulder, his fingertips white as if he's applying force to tell her to remain with her butt on the step.

"I'm a professor," Papa says. "These are my daughters. My youngest is here at my request because her school is closed today. Please feel free to ask me any questions. They're a bit unsettled by everything this morning."

The Gestapo man concedes, speaking only to Papa. The man stands straighter than any man I've seen before. When growing potted trees in our apartment, Papa sometimes will tie a thick stick to their trunk to keep them straight. I wouldn't be surprised if this Gestapo man has one down the back of his shirt and pants.

He asks Papa what he saw, who he saw, if Papa read the leaflet. His voice is just as stiff as he looks.

Papa's answers are expected, safe, and blameless.

On the steps, Angelika has her bottom lip between her teeth, as if she needs to bite down to hold back a smile. The Gestapo man's eyes flick to my sister. He then proceeds to ask Papa the same questions again, only worded slightly differently.

Finally the Gestapo officer takes his stiffness to the next grouping of huddled people.

Papa sits between us again. He grabs my hand, and Angelika's hand, and squeezes. The Gestapo man turns at that moment, his head moving in line with his body. At seeing Papa's unease, he watches us a few moments longer.

I don't like it. I don't like the way his eyes linger on us, narrowed into thin, scrutinizing slits.

But the Gestapo man's eyes go on scrutinizing others.

Time passes. My backside goes numb. Angelika proclaims she's hungry. Who can eat at a time like this, when the entire university is being questioned by Hitler's Gestapo? We're in the teeth of the wolf, trapped. But maybe Angelika feels confident? I've found that the only way to feel confident is to have information. What information is she hiding? Did she know how the entire morning would unfold?

Noise starts above us.

It grows louder.

By the time the noise nears us, I see it's from people standing and moving aside to clear a path down the staircase's middle. We stand as well. Papa edges himself in front of my sister and me.

From the second-floor landing, Sophie emerges on the stairs.

She wasn't successful at getting out of the building, as Angelika had assured herself. My sister stiffens beside me, clearly shocked to see her friend.

Sophie is still wearing a coat. Her face is blank. The suitcase is gone. Her hands are behind her back, my guess in handcuffs. A member of the Gestapo grasps her arm. Behind her is her brother Hans. Their expressions are identical and give nothing away about how they are feeling.

No one says a word.

It's too dangerous to say even a single word.

But Angelika takes a tiny step forward. I pinch her blouse, squeezing the fabric between my fingertips, just the slightest pull to scream, *Don't you dare go any farther!*

We stand there, watching as Sophie is led down the stairs, across the marble floor, then out the university's grand doors. A Gestapo van is outside.

A pin drop could've been heard the entire time.

And Sophie could've been any old girl being taken away. That is, if her gaze hadn't flicked to my sister as she passed us.

I pray no one else witnessed that flick.

CHAPTER 23

Angelika doesn't react. Years of hiding her disability prepared her for the challenge of watching the Gestapo cart away her best friend.

No, Angelika waits to fall apart. She waits for the interrogations at the university to be completed.

Then for the lockdown to be lifted.

Then finally until the safety of our four walls is around us.

That's when my sister breaks. That's when Angelika stops holding back the tears that have hidden in her eyes for hours. I hug myself, watching the pain my sister is in. I want to hug her, too, but she resembles a caged animal, pacing, snarling, crying.

"I need to call Sophie's parents," Angelika announces through her sobs. "They should know she was arrested."

"I'd want to know," Papa says in a soft voice. "But, my petunia, you can't call from here. Why don't I make tea—"

My sister runs toward her bedroom, nothing but heavy footsteps and sobs.

Papa watches her go. "I'll make an early supper."

Or a late lunch, depending on how I look at it. I sink into the couch cushions.

Does it matter how I look at it? No, but it's something to think about besides what happened this morning: the capture of the White Rose. Or some of them at least. But how many are in the resistance group?

How deeply is my sister involved with the group?

Are Sophie and her brother being questioned right now, and will they reveal who else had a hand in their conspiracy?

Are these four walls actually safe?

Tigerlily jumps into my lap, hiccuping my heartbeat. But as soon as she brushes her cheek against my chest, I calm. I give her long strokes, down her head, neck, and back, stopping at her raised tail. She begins to purr, one of the best sounds in the world. The same comforting sound that's always been there.

I notice then that something's missing in our living room. I realize it quickly. The photograph of Mama and Papa from their wedding day isn't on the end table any longer.

From the kitchen, Papa's head keeps turning toward the hallway where our bedrooms are. I bet he has questions for Angelika, too. His head snaps toward our apartment's door. Did he hear a knock?

My hand freezes on Tigerlily's back. She nudges me with her tiny nose, then her whole head.

Papa pulls open the door, but no one is there. He walks out. My eyes don't leave the door. I don't blink. I don't breathe. Until Papa returns, carrying the mail. At a clip, he's flipping through piece by piece.

Papa stops at a white envelope. In his haste to turn it over to open it, he drops it.

Tigerlily startles, then jumps from my lap. "Papa?"

Please don't let it be another leaflet. Not now, not with how combustible everything already feels.

He bends to retrieve the fallen envelope. Mid-crouch he replies, “Uncle Otto.”

What timing. “Can we go to him?”

Before, I didn’t want to leave. But now? Yes. Angelika can’t be in Germany. Sophie and Hans could be saying anything, right this moment.

Papa reads, his head nodding. “Yes. Yes, he’ll be expecting us.” He lets out a breath, then a soft laugh. A relieved laugh is what I think it is, that there’s a solution for all of this. For us, at least. “I have everything we need packed, including Uncle Otto’s telephone number for when we arrive. Angelika and I have papers. You’re too young for papers yet. Get the cat. I’ll destroy this,” he says, holding up the letter, “then I’ll get your sister. Pack anything else small you want. Nothing too noticeable, so that it’s not obvious that we’ve fled. No toothbrushes. We’ll get those once we arrive.” Papa looks at the clock above the sink. “Thank goodness. The afternoon train leaves in just under an hour.”

I’m not surprised Papa has the schedule memorized.

“If we hurry, we can catch it,” Papa says. “But if not, we’ll wait for the evening one. Either way, it’ll be okay.”

I nod briskly, but all the air feels stuck in my lungs.

We are leaving. Within the hour, we'll be leaving. This is the only place I've ever lived, the only place Mama and I existed together. At least we are fleeing to family, to Mama's brother, even if I've never met him. That's something. It's the something that allows me to go to my room and pack those small things. Before, Papa had us pack Bomb Bags. Now, it'll be an Escape Bag.

I pause as my gaze passes over my JM membership certificate on the wall. I don't feel like the same girl who once yearned to join the Hitler Youth. I no longer belong there, at those events, with their ideals, with the other girls. Where does that leave Marianne and me?

I may not know how I feel about her at the moment, but I know I'll kick myself if I forget her face. From the corner of my mirror, I take a photo of us. We stood in line, among soldiers and their families, at one of those photo booths at a festival, a happy day, before all of this, to get a photo together.

I stir at the sound of my sister's voice.

I won't eavesdrop. It's too late for that. I go straight to her room to see what's going on.

"I'm not going anywhere," she says. "Sophie's the first real friend I've had since Johanna. Then after all this happened"—Angelika waves a hand down her left side—"she's the first person I didn't have to hide myself from."

"Besides us," I interject.

Angelika ignores me. "And in return, she trusted me with her own secret. I won't abandon her."

"What can you do?" Papa says. "How can you help her?"

"I don't know. I couldn't do anything for Johanna, but I can do something for Sophie." Angelika shakes her head sharply. "I won't run away."

"You will," he says. Papa isn't a firm man. But today, his tone is like a giant sequoia tree. They date all the way back to the Jurassic period with the dinosaurs. They are tall, strong. Those trees are survivors.

And Angelika listens to Papa, even if there's reluctance as she stands from her bed.

"Pack anything small—"

A loud bang on the door interrupts him.

Normally Tigerlily would find a table or a chair or a

bed to hide under, but I'm stunned when her hair rises and she hisses.

Papa releases an expletive I'd never be able to utter without getting a mouthful of soap. He swallows. I can see his brain working.

He runs from the room, something he can't do if he wants my heart to keep working.

The pounding continues, along with demands for us to open the door.

Papa races back into Angelika's room. "I knew it," he says. "That Gestapo officer seemed too suspicious of me when he questioned me."

"But why?" I ask. "You answered his questions."

"I don't know," Papa replies as he yanks open the trapdoor, the rug moving with the door as one. He drops down his Escape Bag. "But it doesn't matter. Come on," he now whispers, and yanks me by my arm before I have a chance to react.

Before I know it, I'm lowered into the dark cellar. My feet touch the ground. I look up, where my sister eclipses the light as Papa lowers her down next.

“Tigerlily,” I say automatically, without thinking.

Papa releases Angelika, gently, and she favors her left leg. I see he hears me about my cat. He calls for her at a whisper at the exact moment there’s a loud crack.

Angelika gasps. “They broke through the door. Papa!”

Papa’s still above us.

He begins to move, but instead of swinging his legs down toward us, he swings the trapdoor closed.

“Papa!” Angelika and I cry into the darkness.

Chapter 24

No. This can't be happening. Papa is still up there. And he's with whoever barged into our apartment. I picture the Gestapo man from the university, his posture and demeanor both so rigid and severe. Is he inside our apartment? Has he come to question Papa more? Or have they figured out Angelika is connected to the White Rose?

My eyes adjust to the darkness and I search the shadows of Angelika's face for answers to how deeply she's involved, what's happening in our apartment, what's happening to Papa, if we can do anything to help him, how long this will last.

It feels like forever and it's only just begun.

All I can see on Angelika's face is that she's scared.

She trembles beside me. One hand is covering her mouth. Her other is over her heart.

She should be scared. I am. But she should also be angry—with herself.

Papa put himself in the line of fire to keep us safe.

He shouldn't have ever been in a position where he needed to buy us time to hide.

We are supposed to be on a train, toward Switzerland and Uncle Otto.

We are supposed to be distancing ourselves from the White Rose.

Now we're under suspicion for being part of them, because of Angelika. But it's only suspicion. There's no proof to tie us to them, right? Still, I can't help the flare of my nostrils. I also can't help the tears in my eyes.

What is happening to Papa right now?

I picture the Gestapo man again.

The voices above us are muffled.

Footsteps pound around the apartment. There's more than one person here. Maybe three.

There's a thumping sound, as if furniture is toppled. There's a crash and another. There's even more.

Then the noises stop. A door is slammed. All is quiet.

They're gone.

"Papa," I whisper.

I hold my breath, waiting for the trapdoor to open. His face will be there, framed by his mop of blond-gray hair. His blue eyes will be a pool of relief that the Gestapo or whoever was upstairs has left. We'll get on the evening train.

There's no way Angelika can be hesitant to leave now.

I stare at the ceiling, waiting and waiting for Papa.

The trapdoor doesn't open.

I count to sixty. Still, a burst of light never comes.

I count again and again.

Finally I stop counting. Instead I sink to the floor and cry into my knees. Papa would've come for us by now or whispered to us to "hold on" or have done *something* to let us know he's okay.

But Papa isn't okay.

"They took him," Angelika whimpers. "They took him and it's all my fault. Papa didn't only build the trapdoor because of the bombs. He told me he built it because of me, in case they came for me. But he meant my disability. Papa doesn't know all that's going on with the White Rose. Anyone who was involved promised not to tell their family. Not that it mattered. I put you both in danger. They took Papa . . ."

I bite my knee to stop myself from screaming she's right, that it's true, that she put both Papa and me in danger, that Papa is gone because of her. For months, I've feared the Gestapo getting their hands on Angelika. And now it's likely they have our father instead.

"How long," I want to know. "How long have you been involved with them?"

"Not that long. Only these last two leaflets. Sophie didn't even know about the first ones. But when we came back from Ulm . . ." She trails off. "I didn't write anything. I helped, where I could. With the duplicating machine. Getting supplies. Everything had to be bought in small batches. You found the stamps in my room, didn't you?"

"I did."

"Did you tell Papa?"

"No."

"Then Papa should know nothing."

"Are you sure?"

Angelika nods.

Good. They'll interrogate him. But I'm glad I didn't tell him about the stamps. That omission, even if it was accidental, feels like I did something right. I've always felt like I've taken so much from my family. But my omission gives a little something to Papa. He has nothing to say. He's done nothing wrong.

Papa will be home by the morning. I remember something Angelika said about Sophie once, that Sophie was relieved her father was in prison instead of a camp. He could come home from prison.

"But Brigitte," my sister whispers. Her fingers dig into my arm. I'm still bent in half, hugging my legs. "Brigitte, a leaflet . . ." Her voice breaks. "What if they found it?"

I'm confused. "Where?"

"In my room. I brought a copy of the newest one home with me last night."

I straighten so quickly my head spins. "You what?"

She won't look at me. "It hasn't been distributed yet either. Sophie and Hans were supposed to send out the mailing, after the university . . ."

I lick my lips. "But we could've brought a leaflet home, from the university. They weren't mailed yet, but that's how we could have it."

"We have it, though."

And that means imprisonment.

I wipe away a tear so roughly I scratch my own face. "How could you be so stupid, Angelika? Where is it?"

"Hidden. Under my mattress. Maybe they didn't find it."

But we heard all that thumping and slamming.

I close my eyes. I don't trust myself to speak. They have Papa. They better not have the leaflet, too. That leaflet could be the end of our family.

It's all I can think as the hours pass.

I have nothing further to say to my sister.

But she says to me, "We'll freeze down here. Should we go back up? I haven't heard anything in a long time."

Yes, because Papa is gone.

"You're the adult," I say bitterly. Isn't that what she wanted? To be friends with people Sophie's age? To be part of a resistance group? Papa said Angelika was too young for all of that. "You decide."

"Let's go up."

She hoists me onto her shoulders, and I push open the trapdoor. It's heavy and I have to wedge my head and shoulder under it. The weight of the door makes me even angrier at my sister.

Once I'm half in our dark apartment, Angelika shoves and I pull myself up. The door closes as my feet join me. I could leave her down there. But as mad as I am, the thought of being alone in our apartment is too much.

I heave open the trapdoor.

It's not easy, but after Angelika stacks two travel trunks, we are able to get her inside, along with Papa's Escape Bag he dropped down.

I flick on the light.

"No, turn it off!" she hisses, and I'm quick to listen. "No lights. Don't flush the toilet. Don't do anything that could give away we're here."

“So we’re prisoners,” I say, “in our own home?”

But even as I say it, I chastise myself because Papa is in a real one. Papa is in a prison, we’re trapped here, and Papa’s fate could be decided by a single piece of paper.

Chapter 25

Angelika sinks to her knees and shoves her arm beneath her mattress. All I can do is hold my breath and wait to see if the Gestapo has found the leaflet my sister brought home.

Angelika's sudden sob tells me everything I need to know.

I cry, too.

The sound attracts Tigerlily, her head bumping my leg. I hug her against my chest, tears soaking her fur and muffling the sound of my sadness. Holding her makes me realize that if I hadn't called out for Tigerlily, then Papa wouldn't have paused at the trapdoor. Maybe he would've had time to get underground with us. Maybe he'd be here with us now. It's not a good realization.

Not at all. I still blame Angelika. I blame Angelika a lot. But I also blame myself now, too.

From what I can see from the streetlight seeping inside, Angelika's room is a mess. Tigerlily and I quietly examine the rest of the apartment. I start with the front door. Splintered wood is on the floor and the doorknob dangles, letting in light from the hallway, but the door itself is closed. That's a relief. In the kitchen, drawers and cabinets have been left open, the kitchen table lies on its side, and the chairs are askew. Papa's alcove has been torn apart, and a handful of Papa's clay pots are busted. The spilled soil has put a musty smell in the air.

I hear a cough—and I freeze.

It came from the hallway outside our unit.

I creep toward the door, holding my breath, gently stroking Tigerlily's head to keep her calm.

I bend, careful not to touch the door, and look through a gap next to the broken doorknob. It's dark in here but the hallway is lit. It's not a surprise there's a man outside the door, but I still jolt at him standing there, so close that I only see the back of his gray-green pants.

I'm glad I can't see his face.

I take a small step back, then another, and another. My breathing remains shallow as I tiptoe toward Angelika's room again.

She's still crying, stretched out on her belly on her bed.

"Be quiet," I whisper. "There's an officer guarding our door."

Angelika wipes her eyes and forces a swallow. "I bet they're waiting for us to come home. I bet Papa told them we were out."

"What time is it?"

"After curfew."

Without another word, my sister pulls Tigerlily and me into her bed. Her arm goes around us. "I'm sorry," she whispers. "I'm so sorry."

My stomach growls. Hers does, too. I'm worried they'll hear even that. Tigerlily is the only one who had supper. We keep her bowl filled because she yowls endlessly whenever she sees the blue bottom of it.

But we can't risk making noise in the kitchen. All I can do is hope for sleep. Sleep will dull my hunger and pass the time—until Papa is released. He'll talk his way out of the leaflet being in our apartment. He'll tell them what they want to hear. He'll be the perfect Nazi. He's been playing that part for years.

But Papa doesn't come home in the morning. He doesn't come home the next night. A full day passes without Papa, but not without an officer at our door. They rotate. We hear them when they do, and sometimes the men whistle to themselves.

Papa's room is the farthest from the door, but we stay in Angelika's room, in case we need to quickly escape again. We could hide in the cellar a second time, but it's colder, there's no bathroom, and anyone in the building could fetch something they have stored down there and find us.

We go as long as we can without eating or using the bathroom, but we have to begin creeping around the apartment, holding our breaths and pausing whenever the floor creaks. We bring the radio into Angelika's room, too. In the daylight, we crawl, so no one will see us through the windows, the blinds wide open. We can't close them now.

That morning, I'm crawling to check on Tigerlily's food so she doesn't have a meowing fit over a missed breakfast when I hear one of the officers out in the hallway. He's talking with our neighbor Frau Roth, asking her where Angelika and I might be.

"Such good girls," Frau Roth says. "Dedicated to their Hitler Youth activities. I always see Brigitte in her uniform. Angelika once upon a time did, too, but now she goes to the university. Have they not been home? Herr Schmidt usually asks me to water his plants if they're going to be away, which hasn't been for ages."

The officer is slow to answer. Then he asks again, "Do you know where they could be?"

"Well, it's the weekend, so Brigitte probably has a JM event. That girl usually comes home with rosy cheeks from her hikes or a soccer game or something. Angelika doesn't go out as much, but perhaps she's catching a show with friends."

"What friends?"

"Come to think of it, no one comes around much for Angelika. But Brigitte and Marianne are two peas in a pod."

Of course, the officer wants to know everything that Frau Roth knows about Marianne, which is mostly that she's a loud girl. But also that she lost her home in the bombings so she stayed with us for a while.

The officer thanks her, and Frau Roth seems tickled pink she was able to answer his questions. I hear her take a few steps before she stops. "They're not in trouble, are they?"

"If you see the girls," he says, "tell us immediately. Your own safety will be in jeopardy if you do not."

"My safety?"

"Association with anti-Nazis."

Frau Roth gasps. "No, not the Schmidt family. Brigitte—"

"You'll tell us if you see anything."

I don't hear a response. But I picture Frau Roth's shaky nod. Then there's the sound of her footsteps and finally her door opening and closing.

She's spooked.

But how can she not be?

If she sees us, would she turn us in?

I crawl back toward my sister's room. Tigerlily passes me along the way, no doubt going to check on her bowl. Angelika has the radio on low. She's been obsessed with listening, for any news of Papa or Sophie or nearby bombs. If the air raid siren sounds here, we'd have to go to the cellar—and risk being nabbed by the officer. Or we could stay up here—and risk having our apartment crumble down around us. I shudder at both options.

In a whisper, I tell Angelika what I overheard, then say, "After all this time pretending, we've still been marked as anti-Hitler."

Angelika twists her lips. She looks like she's going to say sorry again, but instead she says, "No matter what, we can't let them get their hands on us. We'd be just like the Vogels. You're young enough where they'd send you to a Nazi family to rehabilitate you. But me . . . I'd go to prison. And Papa . . ."

They already have Papa. It's a constant thought in my head. But now I also think about Angelika and me.

At any moment, there's the chance they could hear us. Or they could decide they need to search our apartment again and find us. There's also the small problem that we're almost out of food. With the war rationing, there wasn't much to eat to begin with.

"We need to go," I say. "We need to go to Uncle Otto's, just like Papa planned."

I'm shocked I'm saying it.

Angelika doesn't reply, but she rubs her forehead. "We'd be abandoning everyone. Papa included."

My throat feels swollen. "Papa wants us to be safe. He wants us to go. When he's released, he'll go there, too. Right?"

I hate that I need to ask that question, but I want to hear Angelika say it, that Papa will be released and that he'll come to Switzerland, too.

"Right," she says. I only wish she sounded more confident.

And it's not just Papa. I'll be leaving Marianne, without ever fully revealing everything to her. Without her forgiveness for lying to her. My heart's beating so fast I expect the man outside our door to hear it. "So we go?"

She nods. "In the morning. When everyone is headed to school and work."

I don't sleep a wink.

Then it's Monday morning.

It's hard to imagine leaving the apartment, but I grab Papa's Escape Bag, adding my picture of Marianne, and I carefully tuck Tigerlily inside my rucksack. On Papa's pillow, I leave a note. *Gone to the wedding.*

He'll know what I mean. Anyone else who finds it won't.

"Okay," I say to my sister, trying to infuse my voice with courage that I one hundred percent do not feel. We have our jackets on, bags hugged to our chests. "How do we leave without being seen?" By anyone, even our sweet old neighbor. We can't trust anyone except ourselves. Even that won't come easy after all my sister's lies.

Chapter 26

Our plan is straightforward, yet risky. We can't go out our apartment door. We'd fit through a window, but we'd look like two cat burglars. The trapdoor is the obvious answer.

Down the trapdoor.

Across the cellar.

Out the basement door.

Up the stairs.

That's where things could get perilous. It'd only take a turn of the officer's head to see us from outside our door down the hallway.

And that's exactly what happens when we poke our heads out the basement door into the hallway.

"Run!" Angelika cries.

Within steps, we're across the lobby and barreling

through the door. The sunlight is blinding, and I have to sidestep around someone. That someone is our neighbor Frau Roth, coming in from outside. Her hand goes to her mouth, shock in her eyes.

The officer is yelling for us to stop. The pitch of his voice changes as he barrels outside, too.

"I saw them," Frau Roth squeals. "I saw the Schmidt girls."

Over my shoulder, I watch as Frau Roth latches onto him with both hands. He struggles, yelling at her, but Frau Roth is hysterical. She's beside herself, saying how she's never before seen anybody who's *wanted.*

"Hurry," Angelika says.

I look forward, where we're running. A corner is ahead. Before we reach it, I look behind me one last time. The officer has broken free from Frau Roth's hold. She stands where we nearly bumped into her, hands covering her cheeks, and I see her mouth, *"Go!"*

For once, I'm able to read lips, and I'm glad I can. I'm glad Frau Roth's dramatics were actually to slow down the officer.

We're able to turn down an alleyway before he

rounds the corner. But we keep going as fast as we can. Angelika has Papa's Escape Bag. I have Tigerlily in my rucksack. Both are awkward to carry. Both are heavy. Papa's bag is filled with that money he's been stashing away along with everything we can take with us, and Tigerlily has never missed a meal.

"Hear that?" Angelika says between huffs.

I'm a step behind her. The way she runs may as well be a neon sign that her left side doesn't work the same way as her right. I listen. Voices. Lots of them.

"From the university. We'll hide . . ." After another breath: ". . . in the crowd."

We head that way, and Angelika is right. Something is going on in the square. A big something. We run until we cross into the growing gathering of students and teachers. Then we walk. I try to regain my breathing, finding the only way not to sound like I ran a kilometer is to hold the air in my lungs for a few beats, let it out, hold my breath again. Angelika takes her hat from her pocket and puts it on. Her jacket lining is blue. Mine is black. She turns our brown jackets inside out, transforming them.

"Come on." Angelika leads us toward the same fountain where Marianne and I sheltered against the protest. There, we sit along the edge.

Angelika immediately opens Papa's Escape Bag.

She removes his papers, along with hers.

The identification cards are easy to tear.

Discreetly she drops the remains at her feet.

"Let's go," she says. "Don't look around. It'll only make us seem guilty of something."

Like fleeing a Nazi officer as known anti-Nazis.

"Angelika, how are you going to board a train without your papers?"

She shrugs, trying to appear casual. "If they know my name, those papers will be the end of me. Maybe they won't check. Maybe they'll think I'm under fifteen."

I bite my lip. I don't know. Not with that short hair. Mine's in braids. "What if someone asks us our names?"

"You're Annette . . ." She pauses. "Annette Speer."

I know where the Annette comes from. Hearing it is a mixture of warmth and sadness. "Speer?"

"It's the last name of a man in Hitler's inner circle. I'm Johanna Speer."

I know where that first name comes from, too.

We remain in the crowd, but now that my heart isn't pounding between my ears, I hear what's going on around me. I catch the names *Sophie Scholl*. And *Hans Scholl*. And also *Christoph Probst*, a name new to me.

Angelika hears it, too.

"Excuse me," she says to a girl at random. "What's going on?"

"Protest is about to start."

"Protest?" my sister asks.

"Yeah, against those traitors who went to university here."

Angelika's mouth drops open.

Traitors?

We're in the wrong crowd. A dangerous crowd. How did this same group of students reject what Herr Giesler said only a month ago, but today stand with Hitler, appalled by the White Rose? Is it fear? "Thank you," I say to the girl. Tigerlily mews. I rub my bag, getting an odd look from the girl. "Johanna," I say to Angelika, "we'll miss our train."

Not that I know what time the train is. Not exactly.

But if there's an afternoon and evening train, hopefully there's a morning one we can get, too, if we make it in time.

As we walk, we overhear more. Sophie, Hans, and Christoph are undergoing a trial, that very second. Angelika's feet slow with each new piece of information she picks up.

They've been allowed no visitors.

The apartment that Sophie and Hans share was searched.

Hundreds of unused postage stamps and envelopes were found.

A ledger was also uncovered, with names.

But whose names? Angelika's?

Does it matter? She's leaving.

Papa knows nothing.

Sophie, Hans, and Christoph are being charged with various forms of treason and demoralization of the troops.

The trial is being held at the People's Court at the Palace of Justice.

Angelika's footsteps falter at hearing that.

"What is it?" I whisper.

She stammers, "That—that court. That court is a phony. It's not a fair trial. They only use it to *remove* enemies of Hitler." Angelika shifts herself to face south. "It's only a twenty-minute walk."

"No," I say. "We're going to the train."

My sister begins pulling me. "There's no way we'll make the morning train now. We'll need to wait for the next one, and the station is right by the courthouse."

I don't know if that's true. I've never been to the courthouse.

I find it to be an ornate stone building. A small crowd has gathered outside. While we hid in the swarm of people outside the university, I don't want to do the same here. I tell my sister as much.

"Okay," she says, thinking. "Okay, we'll keep a safe distance."

That ends up being within a bus stop shelter, one where there's a poster of Hitler and the words ONE NATION, ONE EMPIRE, ONE LEADER.

"One hour," I say. I don't know if we even have an hour, but my sister needs that time. I know she does.

If Angelika hears me, she doesn't respond. She stares at the building. It's not as if there's anything to see or anything to overhear. The trial is inside. But my sister feels better about being here. I wish I did. My gaze bounces all around. Down the street. Up the street. People go about their business, but no one bats an eyelash at us. Still, every muscle in my body is tense. I unzip the top of my bag to feel the softness of Tigerlily's fur.

Suddenly, there's a commotion. I shield my eyes against the sun. A man, a woman, and a boy in an army uniform run toward the building. Angelika barely chokes out, "Sophie's family."

Her papa, her mama, her younger brother. They go beyond the two large entry doors.

Angelika uses her sleeve to wipe her eyes. "This is all too much."

It is.

An hour has passed. "Angelika . . ."

"Just a minute more."

It's February. The air is cool. But sweat slides down my back. "You said the train is close by?"

A burst of noise pulls my attention to the courthouse again.

Guards are forcefully shoving Sophie's family back. Her papa stumbles on the steps, trying to reach for Sophie's mama. Her mama is bawling, nearly being carried by the guard, repeating *no, no, no* between sobs. Sophie's youngest brother is stoic. How much has he seen as a soldier in Russia? Then he shakes off the guard and rushes back inside.

"Werner!" Sophie's papa calls. He focuses again on the guard. "When? When is it happening?"

"In a few hours. Five, tonight."

"No!" their mama cries.

"We demand to see Sophie and Hans one last time," Sophie's father says.

I freeze. One last time?

Beside me, Angelika's body slackens. I hold her up, having to drop my bag. Tigerlily doesn't like that. I pull my sister to the ground, then grab my cat before she wiggles from my bag.

At the courthouse, Sophie's family is attracting attention. More people are stopping. People block them from our view. A van pulls up. Sophie's parents are ushered inside. Werner, too, having returned. His voice carries. "I told them to be strong."

I need to be strong, too. For myself, but also for my sister.

"We're leaving," I say. "Which way is the train?"

Angelika's arm rises slowly. She points.

We go that way.

I pray we're not seen. Angelika can't suffer the same fate as Sophie.

At five o'clock tonight, Sophie will die.

The timing of it is a gut punch. Angelika believes the same as Sophie does about Hitler. I do, too. Yet if we get a noon train, we're likely to reach safety in Switzerland just as Sophie loses her life.

CHAPTER 27

I try to stifle the unexpected burst of shame that blooms in me at that thought. I'm running. I feel grateful to be alive. Meanwhile, Sophie is going to die for a belief that we both share. I swallow down the lump in my throat and focus on my sister as we approach the train station. It's only a block more. "Should we walk slower? You're limping."

"I could've tripped and hurt myself," she says. "Not everyone with a limp is disabled, you know. Besides, if we go any slower, we may miss the train."

"I know, I just don't want to draw more attention to us."

"Better?" she snaps.

Her gait is smoother now. Her face shows the effort. But her pursed lips could very easily also be a result of her grief.

I bite the inside of my cheek. "I'm sorry about your friend."

I'm also sorry that Sophie is being called a traitor. And that we can't do anything to help her. It makes me sad to think she's sacrificing her life for the White Rose, when it doesn't seem like anything is going to change.

Angelika curses.

At first, I think it's in response to my apology, but then she does it again. "Look. There's a guard at the station entrance. I bet there's a slew of them inside."

"So what do we do?"

"I don't know." She sidesteps into the entryway of a shop. "We could walk past them. They may not be looking for us here."

I say, "Or they could be."

"But even if they are, would they know who to look for? We could be any two girls."

"Yeah."

"Yeah. We could try. I'm fourteen. You're twelve. Johanna and Annette. That was the plan." Angelika breathes deeply. "But Brigitte, I'm scared."

I take her hand. "I am, too, Johanna."

I mean to lighten the mood, not sure if that's possible, and I get a small smile from my sister. It fades as quickly as it formed. "The judge, the one that presided over Sophie's trial today, he's known for sentencing people to the guillotine." She touches her neck.

A chill runs down my own neck.

The idea of being beheaded is terrifying.

"If I'm caught . . ."

"We won't let that happen," I say. "If a train is too dangerous, we'll find another way. But Papa?"

"Won't be sentenced to the guillotine," Angelika says firmly.

I choose to believe her. I need to. A woman exits the shop we're standing in front of. She grumbles at the inconvenience of having to walk around us.

When she's out of earshot, I say, "We need a new plan."

"We can't go home."

"No," I say, but there has to be someplace else we can hide. Somewhere they won't look for us. "Let's go to the clubhouse."

Who would suspect anti-Nazi girls of hiding in a Nazi building?

It's quiet as we enter the clubhouse through a window. It's daring, doing so in the early afternoon. But we make it. We're in one of the larger meeting rooms.

"You're sure there's no meeting happening today?" my sister asks. She's grimacing.

The walk here took a while, especially with how we dipped into shops whenever we saw an officer. "The next meeting isn't until tomorrow night."

"And we'll be gone by then, once we figure out how." Angelika takes in the room, then drops into a green chair. "This place looks exactly the same."

A few years have passed since my sister's Hitler Youth days, but I bet the furniture has been here longer than us both, along with the paneled walls, the parquet flooring. Once again, Hitler's eyes are on me. "Everywhere we go, he's watching us."

"I've felt that way for a long time. I'm glad you see it now, too, Brigitte."

I'm glad as well, despite the mess our family is in. If only everyone in Germany saw it.

"You know," she says, "it wasn't easy keeping everything from you. You look so much like her."

"Who?" I ask—because I want to hear it.

"Mama." She smiles. I smile. "It sounds silly since you are obviously not Mama and I'm so much older, but I had to stop myself from talking to you like you were her, even before I was involved in the White Rose."

"How, Angelika? How did you even get involved?"

"Well," Angelika says, hugging her left arm across her body in a stretch, "Sophie and I got along right away in Ulm. I told you and Papa that part. It seemed like a stroke of luck she went to the same university. We saw each other there. We started to go to concerts and such. I met her friends. We talked a lot, about what we believed in, our regrets, our hopes. I told you we were like-minded. She never mentioned the White Rose, though. Then one day I overheard bits and pieces of Sophie and Hans exchanging whispers. I asked her about it. Sophie was *very* reluctant to tell me anything."

"But you can be headstrong," I say with a grin.

She nods. "I can be headstrong. I found out that Sophie wasn't even involved until after Ulm, but then she found out what her brother was up to, and she insisted that she help."

"Did she ask you to help, too?"

"No." Angelika shakes her head. "I asked to be involved, in any way I could. Everything was very hush-hush. Very secretive. You have to understand, Brigitte, that I've felt an unsettled pit in my stomach ever since Johanna vanished. But me? I was spared because Hitler approves of who my ancestors are? Because I fit into his master race? Or at least, I did once upon a time."

I don't want to understand my sister's reasoning, but I say, "I understand."

"Thank you," Angelika says, blowing out a long breath. In her chair, she straightens her left leg, and even that causes her nose to scrunch. "Then after I was involved, well, I couldn't talk to Papa or you about it because I needed to protect you. If anyone got taken away, it was supposed to be me. Only me."

"That would've broken our family, too." I add, "I'm glad we're talking now."

There's her smile again. Every time, it's like a gift, a gift that's only mine for a short time longer. Hours have passed since we've learned of Sophie's fate, and the grandfather clock across the room ticks, closer and closer to five o'clock. I'm dreading the melodious chime. Such a beautiful tune is an awful way to proclaim her friend's death.

For now, my sister and I search the clubhouse kitchen for food. I let Tigerlily free, making sure the door of each room we're in is closed. She makes no protest to the canned sardines we find for her. Then Angelika and I giggle when she does her cat business in one of the corners. Better there than in my bag.

We find potatoes. There are always potatoes. Potatoes are encouraged. "Eat them instead of cereals and breads," I've been told by Elisabeth, though my family didn't always obey. "Cereals are imported. Potatoes are homegrown." There's no ration on potatoes.

We boil them, and while we eat, we discuss how on earth we're going to get to Uncle Otto.

"How far of a walk is it?" I ask, shaking my head in

an incredulous way. I mean it as a joke. Switzerland is *days* of walking.

But still, Angelika pulls up the side of her dress. Her hip is swollen and angry looking. "I don't know how far I'll be able to walk."

I wince. Walking is clearly out of the question. But I do remember something, like an itch in my brain. "Remember," I begin, "the day the Vogels disappeared?"

"I try not to."

"I know, but you also said something about smuggling. Smuggling people."

Her face lights up. "Yes. Yes, of course. I bet Manfred would know."

"Who?"

"He let the White Rose use his cellar. That's where the leaflets were duplicated and where the majority of supplies were kept. He has a lot of connections."

"Do you think he's been arrested?"

Angelika bites her lip, but I see the resolve transform her face until her blue eyes are narrowed. "There's only one way to find out. Get the cat."

"Sorry, Tigerlily," I console her as she goes back in my bag.

"I'd suggest you stay here," my sister says. "But I have a feeling you'll say no."

"Bingo."

We consider the window. Getting out will be harder than getting in. "I'll pull over a chair."

My sister nods.

I pass Tigerlily to her.

The grandfather clock ticks, ticks, ticks.

Already, there's less than half an hour until Sophie's sentence will be carried out.

We'll be out of this building and away from the clock before then.

I'm awkwardly shuffling toward the window with the chair when voices funnel into the room. I go still, the chair hovering above the floor.

Angelika stares at the doorway. Beyond the doorway is a long hallway, where on this level there's a second meeting room, the kitchen, a service closet, the bathrooms, then a foyer. People are entering the building.

My arms burn.

Angelika asks, "I thought you said there wasn't a meeting today?"

"There wasn't one I knew of," I whisper. "The window?"

The shake of her head is erratic. "Not enough time."

Angelika surveys the room. It doesn't have a closet or even draperies to hide behind. I slowly lower the chair, being careful not to make a noise.

Tigerlily meows.

"Shh," Angelika says to my cat. And to me, "Follow me."

The soles of our shoes aren't quiet, so we move quickly. I can see my sister is aiming for the kitchen. But the voices grow louder and closer. We only make it to the women's bathroom.

Once inside, I curse the door for not having a lock. Angelika goes straight toward the window. She places my rucksack with Tigerlily in one sink and Papa's Escape Bag in another. She uses the third sink for leverage, groaning as she lifts her body. "The window's been painted over."

She removes a pin that holds back one side of her hair. Angelika begins digging at where the paint of the window meets the windowsill. “It’s working,” she whispers.

“Hurry,” I whisper back.

The voices pass outside the bathroom, going toward the meeting room we were just in. I left the chair in the room’s center, and I hope no one considers its odd placement. I can’t imagine they’d see it there and think: *The Schmidt girls are hiding here!*

But at this point, anything seems possible. Most possible is the fact someone will need to use the bathroom before Angelika is done chipping away the paint.

“Brigitte, help me push.”

I cross to the window, and my palms barely reach the window’s bottom, but I shove with my sister. The paint seal cracks and the window creaks open.

“Thank God—”

Tigerlily meows. But it’s not any meow. It’s loud. She’s a lioness. She’s freed her head from the bag and she’s staring at the bathroom door. She meows again. It’s as if she’s saying, “Someone’s coming!”

Angelika’s face is panicked, her nostrils flared. She grabs my arm. I grab the cat. Before I know it, we’re in a bathroom stall. The door is closed and locked. And there we are, balancing and teetering on the rim of the toilet.

I hold my breath.

The bathroom door opens.

I squeeze my eyes closed because I realize I never grabbed the Escape Bag.

There are footsteps.

Tigerlily shakes loose from the bag in my arms and I whisper-cry, "No!"

It's no use; she disappears beyond the stall we're hiding in.

"Tigerlily?" I hear someone ask outside the stall. My jaw drops, recognizing the high-pitched voice.

Marianne.

Chapter 28

I pause, licking my lips, waiting to see if there are any other voices. Satisfied only my best friend and my cat are on the other side of the stall, I step down from the toilet.

"No," Angelika whispers.

"She'll see our bag anyway."

She already saw Tigerlily. I unlock the door and step into the main part of the bathroom.

"Brigitte?" Marianne says, holding my cat. Angelika is slower to follow. "Angelika? What on earth are you two doing here?"

I'm tongue-tied. I reach for Tigerlily, for something to do in the absence of any words.

Marianne stares at me, at Angelika. She notices our bags. Marianne's mouth drops open. "So it's true?"

I'm not sure how to answer that one either. I pet Tigerlily's head. "What's true?"

"You're anti-Nazi. You're connected to the White Rose. You're on the run from the Gestapo?"

I swallow. "Technically, only Angelika is part of the resistance."

"But the rest?"

I nod.

If she reacted so poorly and so strongly to the leaflet, I can only imagine her reaction to this news. But I'm leaving. I want to come clean. This will likely be the last time I ever see her. I wish I had her pendant to return to her, but I never found it, and now I'll never step foot into my apartment again.

My best friend stands with her back against the door, as far as she can possibly be from me. She says, "Unbelievable. I told them they were wrong. Even with my doubts. There was that leaflet in your house. But no, I told them you only *had* it. Like you said. You only *received* it. I said nothing more. I thought about the trapdoor, but I didn't tell them about that either. I was too afraid to say anything. After Adelita . . ." She lowers her head. “The only thing I said to them was that you were Nazis.”

“Who is *them*?”

“The Gestapo came to my uncle’s. We registered as staying there. And they came to ask me where you could be. I was confused. I’m still so confused. Why are you at the clubhouse?”

I counter, “Why are you?”

“Frau Weber called a meeting. I know you’re not here for that. Why, Brigitte?”

“To hide,” I say. “Until we can leave.”

“Leave?”

“Brigitte,” my sister says, a warning tone in her voice.

She’s right. I shouldn’t say any more than I already have. But I want her forgiveness for lying to her all these months. “It’s not safe for us anymore.”

“Your papa . . .” Marianne glances at me, her back still pressed against the bathroom door. “He was arrested?”

The pain on my face answers her question—just as her body jolts forward as someone tries to enter the bathroom. Angelika dives forward, too, her hip grazing the sink, and holds the door closed.

"Hello?" I hear, coming from the door's other side.

Marianne's eyes go wide.

Her body rocks and Angelika pushes harder against the door to keep it closed.

The voice says again, "Who's in there?" and I realize it's Elisabeth.

Ever so slowly, I shake my head and I mouth, *"Please,"* to my best friend.

Please don't give us away. Please help us. Please do something.

Marianne takes a lungful of air. "It's only me, Elisabeth. I'm sorry. I'm just upset and need a few minutes." She adds, "Alone."

I breathe a sigh of relief. Marianne didn't give us away—not yet anyway. But she truly does look upset, her eyes glossy.

"Is it about your papa?" Elisabeth says. "Let me in."

Marianne yelps, "No!"

It's silent. Until, "Okay, well, you know I'm here if you need me. Like always."

Marianne nods, silently answering her, and I hear footsteps leading away from the door. Elisabeth is gone.

"Your papa?" I whisper.

Her bottom lip trembles and she slides down the door until she's sitting, her knees pulled to her chest. Angelika remains standing beside her, still pressing against the door. But I kneel in front of my best friend. I put Tigerlily down, but she doesn't go anywhere. She rubs against Marianne's leg.

"He's not coming home," Marianne says so quietly I can barely hear her. "He died in Russia."

"No," I say. "I'm so sorry, Marianne."

"I am, too. He died for nothing. Germany is losing. And the Führer . . ."

I take her hands. I'm relieved she lets me.

"Hitler never cared about my papa." She closes her eyes. "Never."

I'm shocked to hear her say it. Absolutely shocked.

She looks at me then. "I read it . . . yesterday's leaflet."

"What? How?" Angelika asks.

"When the Gestapo came to my uncle's, they brought

a leaflet. They said they found it at your apartment. They asked me if I ever saw it before. It felt like a trap. But then they asked me to read it."

I so badly want to ask her what it says. She must recognize the question on my face.

"It said how three hundred thirty thousand of our soldiers died in Stalingrad." Marianne pauses and her nose twitches. "I will never forget that number. My papa is part of that number." Tears fill her eyes now. "The White Rose called their deaths senseless and irresponsible. I didn't understand all of it, but they directed the leaflet toward us students, the German youth, saying we need to get out of the Nazi Party. They said we grew up without ever having opinions of our own."

It's true. It's been true ever since they put a photograph of a Jewish woman on our classroom blackboard and pointed out facial features that were so-called racially impure.

Marianne rubs her nose. Her voice is gravelly as she goes on. "They say the Hitler Youth has drugged us. I can see that now. It took my papa dying as part of those three hundred thirty thousand for me to see it. Over and over again, I was told my papa fought for the good of Germany." Marianne's shoulders begin to shake as tears take her over. "But he died for nothing. No," she corrects, "I can see now that he died for an evil man who compared humans to fleas. How did I not see that as wrong? How did I not see it as wrong that I turned in Adelita? I didn't even think. I just did it, for my own selfish reasons. I feel so guilty about that."

I lean forward to hug her.

Marianne wipes her eyes, but her voice is still ragged. "After I read it, they asked me what I thought of the leaflet. 'You're Germany's youth,' they said, 'do you believe this garbage?'" Marianne shakes her head. "All I could think about was one of the final lines of the leaflet. It said something like 'the dead of Stalingrad implore us to take action.' But I was too scared with him staring at me, so I told him the leaflet was balderdash."

She begins to cry again.

"It's okay," I say. "We pretended, too, for so long."

"I feel ashamed, like I'm letting my papa down."

"Your papa wants you to be safe," I say, thinking of my own and how he sacrificed himself.

"Maybe," she says. "I kept it . . . the leaflet. He was talking to my uncle and I slid it under a book. Each time I read it, it sunk in more and more about how wrong I've been. And how I wish I could do something now to help my papa. But he's gone. It's too late. If only I read these all along, maybe then I would've seen the truth earlier?"

Marianne removes her rucksack from her back and then the pamphlet.

Angelika grabs it. "My god, this may be the only copy left. We duplicated thousands of them the other night, but I bet Manfred got rid of them after everything blew up."

"But we have a copy," I say.

"If only more people could read it," Marianne says. "Maybe they'd see things differently, like I finally did."

If only more people could read it.

"Angelika," I say, "we're going to Manfred's, right?"

"You should call him Herr Eickemeyer. He's an adult."

I nod in agreement as an idea takes shape in my mind. "What if the duplicator is still in Herr Eickemeyer's cellar? What if *we* duplicated this copy and distributed it?"

This idea releases goose bumps on my arm. Hadn't I been sorry that we couldn't do anything to help Sophie? Didn't it make me sad to think she was sacrificing her life for the White Rose when it didn't seem like anything was changing? Well, Marianne changed. More people could change, if given the chance.

But when I look up at my sister, her headshake is furious. "No, that's too dangerous. I won't put you in that situation."

"You're not putting me in it," I say. "I'm putting myself in it. I'm the one suggesting it."

Marianne straightens her legs and stands. She wipes her eyes. I stand, too.

My sister exhales. "It's just too dangerous."

It is dangerous. I wanted to leave to keep my sister from getting caught and suffering the same fate as Sophie. But we should honor the risk Sophie already took. So I tell her, "Sophie won't die in vain. We'll distribute this leaflet for her."

The words sink into my sister's brain. "The three of us?"

I glance at Marianne.

"For my papa," she says. "I want to help, too."

"So it's settled," I say.

Marianne smiles. "It's settled."

Angelika laughs softly. "I guess it's settled."

Tigerlily mews in agreement.

It feels good . . . to have this plan.

It feels good that this plan came from me.

Marianne pokes her head out the bathroom door as the lookout, while Angelika and I open the window as far as it'll go. I shove Angelika through first. She winces and I hate that she's in pain. I hand up Tigerlily, again within the bag she hates so much, along with our Escape Bag. I'm pulled up next, and I pull Marianne out after me.

"What are you going to tell Elisabeth about disappearing?" I ask.

Marianne shrugs. "I was upset and left without telling anyone."

I nod. Makes sense. Elisabeth will think she left by the door, not the window.

Just as we're about to go, I hear the subtle chime of the grandfather clock in the adjacent meeting room. It's five o'clock.

For Sophie, I think. And Johanna. And Marianne's papa. And for so many others.

I say, "Let's go."

Chapter 29

Never before have I felt closer to Mama. During Germany's first war, she ran toward the grocery store to take a stand against the food shortage. Now, with the leaflet hidden in Papa's Escape Bag, we run toward the duplicator.

Or at least we hope the duplicator is still at Herr Eickemeyer's.

The sun remains bright, but it's lower in the sky.

Angelika says, "We'll need to hurry. Curfew is only in a few hours."

Herr Eickemeyer's row home isn't far. We arrive within five minutes. Angelika knocks at his door. Marianne and I grasp hands, the moment feeling like it calls for it. I almost can't believe she's come with us.

Herr Eickemeyer could be at the market or otherwise

not home. He could be in prison. He could answer. And if he answers, then we could officially be part of the resistance against Hitler. My palms are sweaty.

He answers. Or at least a young man answers. I'm not certain it's Herr Eickemeyer until he says, "Angelika?" Before she can reply, his gaze darts up and down the street and he ushers her inside.

"My sister and her friend," Angelika says when his eyes pause on us. It's almost like his eyeballs say, *Aren't they a little young to be running around with you and coming here?*

And quite frankly, it's not an absurd thing for him to think. Papa said Angelika was too young—at nineteen—to run with girls like Sophie. So who do I think I am—still another month until I'm even a "teen"—to be doing something so daring?

Inside, he asks my sister, "Are you girls in danger?"

"Yes and no," Angelika says.

Herr Eickemeyer twists his lips. "Explain."

"No one's chasing us . . . at the moment. But they've arrested our father and I think they've made a connection between me and the White Rose." She pauses then. "Should I not have come here? I'm sorry, I wasn't thinking, beyond that you may know how to smuggle us out of München."

"And that you may still have a duplicator thingy," Marianne adds.

He glances at Marianne, his forehead creased. He startles when my bag meows. I unzip it so Tigerlily can see what's going on in the room, which looks more like a work space than a living space. Herr Eickemeyer must be an architect. The room is filled with big tables, blueprints, storage tubes, fancy lamps, rulers, and a typewriter.

Poor Herr Eickemeyer is overwhelmed, but he says to Angelika, "Your timing couldn't be better. Klaus, Ingrid, Rudolf . . . they're in the cellar. They told me about Sophie, Hans, and Christoph." He checks his wristwatch. "I've got a truck coming in an hour. There's room for you three to hide in the back of the truck, too, if you squeeze. But we'll need a larger bribe."

"We have money," Angelika says. "And it's only my sister and me."

"And my cat," I say.

"I'm staying," Marianne says. "I'm here for the machine."

I can't help my smile. Marianne's always been single-minded—and it sure feels good to be like-minded again.

"What's she talking about?" Herr Eickemeyer asks.

Angelika removes the leaflet from her bag. "We have this."

His eyebrows shoot toward the ceiling. "How'd you come upon that? I destroyed the ones for today's mail."

"I took one home with me the other night. It got taken by the Gestapo." She gestures in a circular motion. "The leaflet's transferred hands a few times. But we have it. Do you still have the duplicator in the cellar?"

He nods toward the corner. "I moved it up here, in case they put two and two together and searched my flat. It would've been odd for me to have it down in the cellar. But up here . . ."

It fits right in among all his work things. There it is, the duplicator machine.

"Can we use it?" my sister asks. "Before we leave?"

Herr Eickemeyer rocks back onto his heels, his hands deep in his pockets. "Girls—"

I'm quick to say, "We don't want Sophie—or anyone else involved—to die in vain."

The line works on Herr Eickemeyer, too. He sighs but only says, "Hurry."

Angelika does. "I'll cut a stencil."

I don't know how any of it works, but Angelika explains. She'll use the typewriter, with a special attachment, to retype the leaflet. That'll produce a stencil we'll use with the duplicator. There's a crank, and when it's turned, the ink from the stencil is pressed onto a piece of paper.

I can't believe we're doing this. Mama would be proud. So would Papa. I hope he's okay. Better yet, I hope he's already free, en route to see my note on his pillow.

Angelika settles at the typewriter.

Marianne says, "It feels good to do something, just like the White Rose wanted."

Her words spin in my head, my own words forming. "At the top of the leaflet," I begin, "can we add something? Can we add something like 'despite everything, their spirit lives on'?"

Angelika smiles. "Oh yes, we can."

My sister may not have been able to help Johanna all those years ago. But this is something she can do for Sophie. She gets to typing.

Herr Eickemeyer paces, cradling Tigerlily in his arms and periodically checking a window. "I got rid of all the stamps and envelopes, too. It would've looked weird if I had thousands."

"We can go get more," I say.

"No, too risky. I can't have people coming and going from here this late. The three of you don't exactly look like clients. It could attract attention and jeopardize getting you girls out of here safely. But," he says, "I've got maybe twenty or so of each that I have for normal business purposes. They're yours."

We thank him in unison, smiles creeping onto our faces at our combined voice.

Soon, we have a stencil.

Angelika cranks, copying the White Rose's words one paper at a time.

I blow on the ink, drying it. Every time I see the message we added at the top, my heart quickens.

DESPITE EVERYTHING, THEIR SPIRIT LIVES ON.

Yes, it does.

And I imagine the livid response from the Nazis. They thought by capturing Sophie and Hans, they put a stop to the leaflets. Think again.

Once the leaflet is in an envelope, Marianne adds a stamp.

After the day we've had and the exertion of making the leaflets, Angelika is exhausted, but her brain is still turning. She says, "Let's be strategic. Barrooms and taverns, like before? But maybe other cities, too? When we mailed the last leaflet, Sophie took a train to Hamburg and mailed from there. It made the resistance look bigger, like we'd spread to cities beyond München. And then we actually *did* expand. Hans told us that resistance groups have begun in Berlin, Freiburg, Hamburg. We should mail to those cities to let them know the White Rose spirit lives on."

"And newspapers," I suggest. "Maybe someone will be brave enough to reprint it. Then imagine how many people the leaflet could reach."

We have a plan, but we still need addresses.

Angelika says, "The White Rose didn't keep addresses. Too risky. A phone book was used each time."

"Do you have one?" I ask Herr Eickemeyer.

"There's no time," he says. "Truck will be here in five minutes. I'm about to go below and get the others."

"I'll get them," Marianne says. "The addresses, I mean. I'll use my uncle's phone book and then I'll drop the envelopes in any old mailbox."

"No," I say as Herr Eickemeyer heads for the cellar stairs and Angelika begins shoving the envelopes into a bag. I wish we hadn't stuffed the envelopes yet. I wish they were still empty. "That's too much to ask of you, Marianne."

"I want to." There's so much determination in the slight raise of her chin. "Like I said, for my papa."

"But also for you," Angelika suggests. "Both of you have been brainwashed since you were practically babies."

Marianne gives a slow nod. “I want to make my own choices. You can trust me.”

Angelika squeezes her arm. “We trust you. We’ll take one with us, too, in case someone is monitoring the mail now. Here’s the rest.”

“But,” I ask my best friend, “what if you get caught?”

“I’ll tell those buttinskis to mind their own business.”

“I’m being serious.” But hearing her say that word warms me. It reminds me of the Jungmädel Challenge and how Marianne was there for me then, like she’s here for me now.

“I’ll be careful, Brigitte. It’s you I’m worried about. How long will you be gone?”

“I don’t know.”

“Can you at least tell me where you’re going?”

I can, because I trust her, too. I trust my best friend so much. “Switzerland.”

Marianne’s mouth drops open. “You’re leaving Germany?”

“It feels scary,” I admit, especially with Papa still here and his fate still unknown.

“It feels far,” she says.

"I'll write you as soon as I can."

She nods. I know she wishes she could come, but we're leaving *now* and her mama, brother, and sisters are obviously not here. I also don't know how her mama feels about Hitler.

Herr Eickemeyer returns with two older boys and a girl. My guess is they are in their early twenties. They don't seem surprised to see Angelika, but they look at Marianne and me oddly.

"All right," Herr Eickemeyer says. "Truck will be here in sixty seconds."

I throw my arms around Marianne, whispering into her ear, "I have the picture of us, from the photo booth."

"Promise me there'll be more festivals."

"Promise," I say. Herr Eickemeyer hands me Tigerlily. As soon as she's in my bag, it's clear from her mewling she's unhappy.

Angelika and Marianne hug, too, and Herr Eickemeyer gives strict instructions. "Everyone go out at the same time. Marianne, go to the right. Don't look back. Don't stop walking. Get home before curfew. All those addresses can wait until tomorrow. The rest of you, go straight into the back of the truck. No talking. No dillydallying. We've got one try at this."

I could throw up.

I hold Tigerlily against my chest, waiting for Herr Eickemeyer to open the door.

"Go, go, go," he whispers.

We run into the night. The pickup truck slows to a stop. It's smaller than I expected, where we'll have to lie on our bellies within the truck's bed. It doesn't look like it could fit multiple people, which I suppose is the point. Marianne goes to the right, the bag with our illicit leaflets over her shoulder. We run over the cobblestone toward the idling vehicle. Herr Eickemeyer pulls aside a flap. The others climb in. Angelika pushes me forward. I can't help one last look over my shoulder. Marianne's walking at a clip. She doesn't look back. I'm inside, then Angelika. My sister lets out a long breath. The flap closes. And then we're moving, tires bouncing over the cobblestones away from everything I know.

Chapter 30

For the past hour, while we prepared the leaflets, then raced into the back of this pickup truck, adrenaline fueled me. Now, in the dark, the space so cramped that half my body overlaps my sister's, that adrenaline runs out and panic takes over.

It's dark.

Not a sliver of light.

I breathe the same air, again and again.

The smell of manure—most likely carried in this truck prior to us—burns my nose.

We rumble down the road, the engine so loud I can barely hear myself think.

Barely.

But I do.

I think about Marianne, and if that backward glance

will be the last time I see her. I worry about her getting stopped on the way home. I worry about her making it to her uncle's before curfew. Then I worry about tomorrow, when she mails the leaflets. But I feel confident that if anyone can do this, it's Marianne.

I think about Papa, and how each bump of this truck takes me farther from him. Tears leak from my eyes. We left him in a prison, with no idea what will happen to him. If the smell of the manure didn't already hitch my breath, that thought surely does.

I think about the bombs, and if they'll hit München again, destroying all the places that my memories are built from. It's the only place I've ever called home. It's Mama's city.

Tigerlily expresses her discomfort from time to time, but otherwise, we're all silent in the truck. It's for the better. If I open my mouth, only sadness will tumble out.

As the hours pass, all that sustains me is the thought that I'm going toward family. Mama's family.

Abruptly, the pickup stops. When the flap is pulled aside, it reveals more darkness. Klaus and Rudolf get out first, helping Ingrid, me, then Angelika. A raspy voice tells us, "Swiss border is straight ahead over a stone wall. That's the easy part. Now listen, you young folks need to get at least ten kilometers farther before anyone catches you or else you'll be sent back as fugitives. My advice, don't let them catch you even after ten kilometers. You're not fugitives at that point, but refugees—and illegal foreigners are placed in internment camps until this godforsaken war ends."

I panic at that word. *Camps*.

Angelika finds my hand in the dark and squeezes it.

The faceless man continues, his explanation sounding practiced, as if he's done this before. "It's my hope you have host families lined up. Get there. Get there fast. If you don't, board a train that'll take you deep into the country and seek asylum. Now go."

We go, no questions asked. We go as fast as we can toward that stone wall. Within thirty breaths of leaving the truck, I'm on the Swiss side. Crossing into Switzerland feels comically easy, with only a waist-high amount of stone distancing us from Hitler's Germany.

But we could be sent back—as runaways.

We run deeper into the quiet forest, only the owls greeting us, as if asking who's there. Angelika trips over a root and Klaus silently helps her up. We don't talk; we focus on going those ten kilometers, the terrain not making it easy with its steep slopes. We find it easier to slide down on our backsides. When we go up, there are large rocks to hold on to. The smell of the water isn't far away.

I wear the rucksack with Tigerlily on my back, having to lean forward to better support her. My back aches, but I know Angelika has it worse. She cringes with every step.

Finally, Klaus says, "I think we've gone the ten."

We let out a breath, all together. It's been two hours since we climbed over the waist-high wall and we picked our way through the early morning. A red glow begins to break through the trees. But there's still farther to go.

We reach a village soon after. No one bats an eyelash at us, as if they see dirty, desperate-looking people stumble down their streets every day. They probably do. Outside a general store, Angelika can barely stand,

and it's decided I should go inside to call Uncle Otto. The store owner's face relaxes when I ask to use his phone, as if he's relieved I have someone to call.

"Uncle Otto," I say once he's on the telephone line.

"Angelika?" he asks.

"Brigitte," I correct.

"Of course. You sound so much like your sister. She's with you?"

"Yes," I say. "I'm sorry we arrived late, but we're finally here. For the wedding."

"Yes, yes, of course. I've been expecting you. I'm on my way."

"No," I say. We're not at the train station like planned. Instead I tell him, "We've stopped for food at . . ."

The store owner chimes in with his address.

"I'll be there within an hour," Uncle Otto assures me, but there's concern in his voice.

He's here in forty minutes.

When Uncle Otto arrives, he swoops me into his arms so quickly that I don't get a chance to look at him. But at once, I feel safe, I feel loved, I feel Mama's love in him.

Then I see her in him in the form of Mama's chin dimple. I only ever saw it in photographs. Now I see it on Uncle Otto's welcoming face. Once he's had a good look at me—he's never seen me in person either—he wraps Angelika in a hug. "Where's your father?" I hear him say.

Angelika only shakes her head.

Uncle Otto's eyes close. "All right." He glances at Klaus, Ingrid, and Rudolf. "We'll figure everything out."

It sounds so much like Papa that his words are a sharp pain in my heart.

"And you've brought friends," Uncle Otto says. "Best to all hurry and get back to the farm."

How different it is in this truck, sunlight streaming through the windows, surrounded by mountains, fresh air filling my lungs. Only hours away, it's the same mountain air I breathed in Germany. The same air I breathed on my JM trips. Yet I feel a million kilometers away, not a plane in the sky to drop their bombs on us. Here, we'll be free.

Epilogue

It's been two years since we arrived on Uncle Otto's farm.

Slowly, Angelika's bruises faded.

After a time, Klaus, Ingrid, and Rudolf moved on.

But still, there's been no word from Papa.

There was a time when I so badly wanted to be part of something. I had thought my answer was the Hitler Youth. But now I only crave my family being whole again.

A desperation that only becomes sharper because of the bombings.

München was hit again, eight months after we fled. Then again six months later. Then three months after that. In my mind, I imagined a city of rubble, with only Papa's prison and Marianne's apartment still standing.

After each air raid, I wrote Marianne. Every time, I've told her to come here, but each of her replies says how her mama won't hear of it. It'd be too hard for a family the size of theirs. Plus Marianne's mama says her husband died for Germany and Germany is where they'll remain.

But what of my papa? That unknown is unbearable. Uncle Otto sought out whatever information he could find for us, using the radio, the newspapers, and writing letters. We learned that over a hundred people connected to the White Rose were arrested and imprisoned. There was apparently a professor who helped write one of the leaflets. He was executed the same way as Sophie. His wife and sister, having had zero involvement, were jailed. They took his twelve-year-old daughter and put her under the care of the Gestapo.

That could've been me.

I'm fortunate. So many others are not.

After Sophie's trial, there was a second trial. That was when the professor was sentenced to the guillotine, along with two others. Ten more received prison terms. One person was let go.

I prayed and prayed that person was Papa. Every day I sit on the farmhouse steps, staring out at the horizon, hoping to see Papa. But the days, weeks, and months have passed and he hasn't come. Papa would come if he could.

My prayers are now pleas . . . that perhaps he's within the hundred arrestees who are awaiting trial. And perhaps that trial will never come.

There's a chance of that.

Last summer, in August 1944, the Allies, the countries who banded together against Hitler's war, won back Paris.

Maybe the Allies will take over München and the rest of Germany.

Uncle Otto says he feels the tides are turning. Angelika smiles at me and says how we had a hand in it because of what we did with that final leaflet.

That final leaflet. When I think about it now, I get goose bumps both from the danger that was involved and also the waves it caused. Those goose bumps are the positive kind. I was part of something good, if only for an hour.

Thanks to Marianne, the leaflets went out in the mail. They reached everywhere we wanted them to reach—and beyond. In fact, the leaflet Angelika smuggled out with our spur-of-the-moment message at the top reached all the way to London. Then I couldn't believe it, but the British Air Force swapped their bombs for our leaflets and dropped them from their planes all over Germany.

Sophie's spirit lived on and on and on, wherever the breeze took it. Sometimes I think I can feel it here. Uncle Otto said it was felt, even, in the concentration camps. Word of the leaflets filtered through the chain-link fences, telling those who were trapped that there were people taking a stand against Hitler. I hope the news also reaches Klaus, Ingrid, and Rudolf wherever they are in Switzerland's mountainsides.

When news comes in April that Adolf Hitler took his

own life, I'm not the least bit sad. In fact, Angelika and I twirl around Uncle Otto's kitchen.

"The wolf is dead!" she cheers. Hitler ruled all my life. At the age of three, I was told my race was the master one and that Jews were the enemy. I hope the fighting will end now. I hope those beliefs will be wiped out. It's been at the cost of so many. My sister says, "It won't be long now until this war is over."

And she's right. A few days later we learn that Germany surrenders.

Germany surrenders.

The war is over.

The Allies have control of the cities, of the concentration camps, of the prisons.

Papa . . .

On Uncle Otto's front steps, I let my fingertips graze the chamomile flowers. The white petals and yellow center of the flower once reminded me of the white shirts and blonde hair of my fellow JM members. Now it's impossible for me to see them and not think of Papa and his nickname for Marianne. He gave it to her because her belongings spread like the flower around our apartment. But in the end, it was Marianne who helped spread the White Rose's message. I like that better, I think, as I stare at the horizon as I always do.

But today, a figure appears. It's mirage-like, fuzzy around the edges.

I squint.

The figure—a man—comes closer.

I stand.

I descend the steps.

The stone walkway is hot beneath my bare feet. The August sun is high in the sky. With my hand, I shield my eyes. Then it's as if my heart leaves my body and sprints toward the man. Toward Papa.

It's him!

"Angelika!"

I'm already crying by the time she barrels outside. "What is it?"

"Who!" I say. "It's *who*!"

Then I'm running toward Papa. Angelika is beside me. Uncle Otto appears from the barn, Tigerlily on his heels. A knowing smile appears on his face and a laugh sprouts on his lips. It's the kind of laugh that takes over the entire body. I decide Mama must've laughed in that same funny way.

Papa's arms are already stretched wide, awaiting his flowers. Papa is free. We're all free. The feeling is gloriously new, new, new.

A NOTE FROM THE AUTHOR

Dear reader,

Thank you for traveling back to the early 1940s with me, to a time in history that I wish was fictional but was sadly very real. The White Rose resistance was real. Sophie Scholl and Hans Scholl were real. So were their tragic deaths on February 22, 1943.

The White Rose was a nonviolent movement led primarily by students, who wrote and circulated six anti-Nazi leaflets totaling about fifteen thousand copies. My goal was to bring to life the efforts of the White Rose, through the eyes of Brigitte, a fictional character who was raised during a time when she didn't know any different than the Nazi Party's way of life. Slowly, her eyes are opened, in part due to her sister, whose character is also fictional.

While Angelika's role in the White Rose is

fabricated, Sophie's secretive nature and Angelika's limited involvement allowed me to feel comfortable adding Angelika as a fictional member of the White Rose resistance group. In reality, the White Rose included a known twenty-four members. And my research indicated that more than one hundred people were arrested and/or imprisoned during the Gestapo investigation of the White Rose leaflet campaign.

I felt so saddened learning of the fate of Sophie and the other White Rose members, but I was encouraged to learn that Sophie was honored with a slogan that appeared on the walls of the university: SCHOLL LIVES! YOU CAN BREAK THE BODY BUT NEVER THE SPIRIT! The White Rose's final pamphlet was also circulated even after their arrests and executions, with the addition of the phrase DESPITE EVERYTHING, THEIR SPIRIT LIVES ON. This line was actually added by Hans Leipelt and Marie-Luise Jahn. I want to ensure they receive credit, but I gave Brigitte, Angelika, and Marianne the privilege and honor of doctoring the final leaflet, which was circulated throughout Germany and also smuggled out of the country. A brave man named

Helmuth James Graf von Moltke, a founding member of a resistance group known as Kreisau Circle, completed this heroic act, and I'd like to make sure he also receives credit as the one who smuggled the final leaflet from Germany. Within the novel, it felt fitting to let Angelika complete the act while she honored the memory of Sophie. The smuggled leaflet eventually reached England, where British warplanes dropped the leaflet, then titled A GERMAN LEAFLET: MANIFESTO OF THE MUNICH STUDENTS, over German cities and towns. (München is spelled Munich in English.)

During the 1940s, people didn't know the extent of details about poliomyelitis (polio disease) that we know now, including whether polio was hereditary (the earliest studies I found occurred in the 1950s) and if the virus could return (post-polio syndrome wasn't identified until the 1980s). I believe these unknowns about the disease would've created a lot of uncertainty and fear about Angelika's well-being and safety. During Adolf Hitler's rule, four hundred thousand (known) people were sterilized against their will.

In 1945, during the final days of the Second World War, some White Rose prisoners were still awaiting execution. They were freed by Allied troops after Germany's surrender. In my novel, this is when Brigitte's papa was released from prison.

I did my best to align my novel's story line with the real-life timeline of the war and bombings, the mailing of the White Rose pamphlets, and other historical events, such as the assemblies, the protests, and the execution of Sophie and Hans. Whenever possible, I incorporated historical details, though liberties were taken from time to time to further build the novel's plotline. One such example is how I am uncertain if Sophie participated in the speech-turned-riot in January 1943. However, since she was a student of the university, I found it plausible she was in attendance. Hundreds of people poured into the streets and marched that day. Another instance of fictionalizing details occurs on the day Sophie distributed the final leaflet at the university. A janitor named Jakob Schmid was the only person who reported seeing Sophie distribute the leaflets.

However, I placed Brigitte in the university so that we could see the event unfold through her eyes.

I made these decisions for the purpose of storytelling. In these scenes and throughout the novel, any remaining inaccuracies are my own. To my authenticity readers, thank you for lending your eyes and brains with regard to details relating to the White Rose, World War II–era Germany, and persons with disabilities. Your help was invaluable.

When researching the novel, the following are some of the books and films I relied on to gain a better understanding of the White Rose and Nazi Germany:

- *White Rose* by Kip Wilson (fiction, ages 12+)
- *The White Rose: Munich, 1942–1943* by Inge Scholl (nonfiction, no age rating)
- *We Will Not Be Silent: The White Rose Student Resistance Movement That Defied Adolf Hitler* by Russell Freedman (nonfiction, ages 10+)
- *Sophie Scholl: The Final Days* (film, ages 16+)
- *Fanny's Journey* (film, ages 13+)

I hope you'll be encouraged to learn more about these brave young heroes. As Thomas Mann (novelist and winner of the Nobel Prize for Literature) said of the White Rose members, "Gallant, glorious young people! You have not died in vain. You will not be forgotten."

The White Rose will be remembered for their words. They've shown us how powerful words can be.

Best,

J Walsh

ABOUT THE AUTHOR

JENNI L. WALSH is the author of the She Dared books: *Bethany Hamilton* and *Malala Yousafzai*. She also writes historical fiction for adults. Jenni's passion lies in transporting readers to another world, be it in historical or contemporary settings. She is a proud graduate of Villanova University and lives in the Philadelphia suburbs with her husband, daughter, son, Newfypoo, and tabby cat (who inspired Tigerlily). Learn more about Jenni and her books at jennilwalsh.com.